Book of Puppet Plays for the Christian Year

(including detailed instructions on
How to make a giant Puppet Theatre)

Suitable for Ages 8+

By

Jon & Fiona Hamer

Acknowledgements:

Sincere thanks for all the ideas, enthusiasm and delivery of these plays must be given to the children of the St Catherine's Sunday School including Ben H, Emily R, Ruby G, Alex H, Amy C, Emily K, Theo W, Ed G, Bobby K, Arthur W and Emily M.

Appreciation must be given to their parents who have listened to the perfectionist practising of their lines to "get it right for the big day".

Thanks also to our clergy who have always supported this type of ministry and who have always been highly appreciative of the performances. And lastly a big thank you to our very supportive church family at St. Catherine's.

The tunes for the songs can be found in most hymn books.

First published in 2018 by Kindle Direct Publishing

© 2018 Jon Hamer

The right of Jon Hamer to be identified as the author of this work has been asserted by him in accordance with the Copyright Designs and Patent Act 1988

ISBN 9781520447032

Contents

Introduction

My wife and I attend St Catherine's Church, Preston- next- Faversham, Kent. As with many churches, St Catherine's did not have an issue with attracting parents with young children to the church but it did have a problem with the engagement and retention of children as they grew up. The contemporary church may be seen by many to be out of touch, locked in the past with a solemn and serious religious backdrop. If we believe that children learn through playing and that most messages are understood through conversation and retained through a fun environment, then a different approach is needed for children in the modern church.

Like many churches, St Catherine's children were sent to Sunday school and returned quietly half way through the service and left again once the service had finished with very little interaction with the congregation. At successive Parochial Church Council meetings, the agenda item of Sunday School was addressed. At one point during these meetings it was stated that if we wanted children in the church in future then we should not be bundling them off and effectively segregating them from the main congregation. What we needed to do was to put children on view, "front and centre", so that the church could come together as a community encompassing all ages.

It was decided that one of the best way to keep children interested and learning within the church was through puppets. Members of the congregation were asked to sponsor a puppet in order to buy them however there were still two problems:

1. there were no books of plays to purchase that were ready to perform and

2. we couldn't find any plans anywhere on how to make a Puppet Theatre large enough for 4 children to work side by side.

So, we wrote the plays, made the Puppet Theatre and bought the puppets. We then decided that other churches could benefit from what we had done and have published this book.

In this book, we provide some of the puppet plays that have been written for and with the children of St Catherine's Church. We have had a lot of fun writing them, the children have had a lot of fun performing them and it *has* been said that the congregation listen more to the plays than the sermons.

We have also found that getting children to periodically perform with puppets in front of a congregation, allows them to be confident when giving public performances which is a life skill in itself. The plays themselves are light hearted and often based on bible stories and some have songs set to popular hymns with the words changed. As Christ taught, children are very important in the Church and it is in the Church's interests to make sure that children are retained. This book will no doubt help in that endeavour.

Foreword

Young people have a happy knack of putting into words what older people sometimes think but don't say. At other times they notice things that are important but others overlook. In worship too, they have their own thoughts and questions about God, which highlight areas of faith and make us all think.

In these plays, puppets take on a life of their own but I suspect our young have enjoyed putting words into their mouths. Dartford people might not want to be associated with a donkey but then again, donkeys do have a place in both the Christmas and Easter stories. Whitsun (Pentecost), Mothering Sunday, Harvest Festival (who would have pictured Harvest in Iceland with just fish?) are also captured here. Brussel sprouts get a mention (well deserved, I think). And Herod as Scrooge – pure genius to make the Dickens characters of "A Christmas Carol" slip into those involved in the characters from the gospel story of the birth Jesus. And as for merging a Christmas day family setting with the story of the Prodigal Son (or in this case daughter) - that was rather illuminating.

Read on and enjoy – but beware of the parrot!

The Venerable Peter Lock

Tips for Great Puppet Plays

Don't do a play every week but leave them for special occasions.

Make sure the child opens the puppets mouth as they are speaking the lines. Nothing looks worse than lines being spoken and the puppets being inanimate.

When two puppets are clearly supposed to speaking to each other, have the children make the puppets look at each other.

Use props like microphones (e.g. percussion beater wrapped in tin foil) to add life to the characters.

Have the church invest in some mobile microphones that the children can wear. The biggest complaint we had in the early days of puppet plays was that the elderly could not hear them very well which was quite frustrating for them.

Children have a habit of speaking very quickly and their lines will be difficult to hear in a church because the words may run into each other with the echo. Make sure the child is speaking relatively slowly.

If you have a child who speaks softly when reading their part, ask them to shout the lines at you like when they are shouting at their brother or sister – that usually increases the volume!

When rehearsing, as a teacher - move away from the theatre and ask the children to keep speaking more loudly so you can still hear them.

If there is a joke in the script, make the child pause after delivery of the joke (only for a second) then the congregation has a chance to digest the joke and enjoy it.

Always give praise to the child when they do something right and remember that the puppet theatre is a treat for them and not preparation for the Royal Academy of Dramatic Arts. Make it fun – lots of fun!

Where there is a narrator part, this does not need to be voiced from within the puppet theatre – it can be voiced by a child (with or without a puppet) or by an adult next to the theatre to offer some support if they are nervous.

The words in brackets in the scripts give information/stage direction and are not supposed to be spoken by the puppeteer.

Print the scripts single sided so they can be pinned to the Plinth in front of the puppeteer. As the play progresses, each used page of the script can be ripped off the pin

SAFETY: Additional stability should be provided to the Puppet Theatre by putting some weights on the Side Frames prior to use of the Puppet Theatre by children.

How to Make a Puppet Theatre

Resources:

Wood: cross section 4.3cm²:	14.1m
9 mm Ply Wood:	1.6m x 0.4m
13mm Pine:	1.3m x >0.14m
Self-drill wood screws:	3cm & 4cm
8cm Hinges:	x4
1cm diameter dowel:	4.5m
Calico Backdrop:	1.35m x 0.65m (hem additional)
Heavy cloth:	1m x 2m (for lower part of Front Frame)
	1.42m x 1m (for each lower Side Frame)
Light cloth:	1.5m x 1m (for each upper Side Frame)

Tools:

Quick grip clamps x2	Paints for wood and fabric with
Electric Screwdriver/ Drill	associated primers
Tenon saw	Mallet & Wood Chisel
Mitre block	Fine tooth electric jigsaw
12mm Spade drill bit	Scissors
Various grades of sandpaper	Paint brushes
Set square	Sharp pencil

Notes

- The Puppet Theatre will comfortably accommodate 4 children side by side with puppets.
- It is very useful to have 2 people making this Puppet Theatre but it can be done with one person.
- All cuts in wood are to be made using a tenon saw and mitre block to keep edges straight.
- Fabric does not have to be hemmed as it can be folded and stapled to prevent fraying. Having said that, it is easier if the material is hemmed.
- Be careful of the overall height of the Puppet Theatre. As a minimum it needs to be able to fit through your doorways! If it is too high, you can always reduce the height by shortening the Uprights to the desired length.
- The amount of time to make this will from course vary from person to person however the Puppet Theatre should be able to be assembled within 6 hours. Painting the Header Board and Backdrops perhaps another day.

INSTRUCTIONS

Cut 1 length of 4.3cm² to a length of 162.2cm. At a distance of 88.8cm from one end of the wood, make a cut 2.2cm deep. Make a second cut at 93.2cm at a depth of 2.2cm. Chisel out the 4.4cm of wood to make a channel as shown in the inset picture below. Make a third cut, 8cm from the end of your piece of wood at a depth of 2.2cm and a fourth cut at 12.4cm from the end at a depth of 2.2cm. If your wood is wider, make you first cuts at 88.8cm and 8cm from the ends and increase the width of the second cuts to accommodate the width of your wood. Make two of these pieces – PART A.

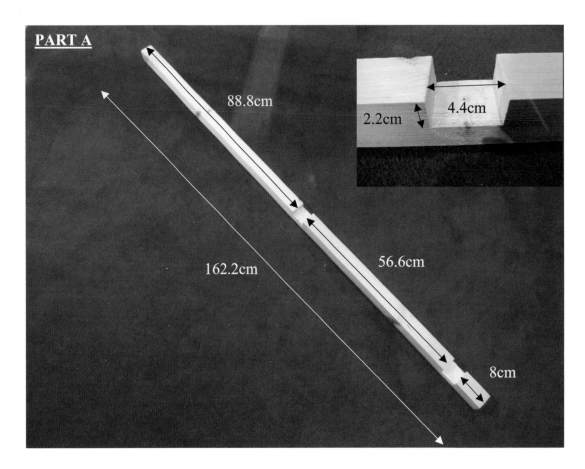

Cut a second length of wood 4.3cm² to a length of 76.3cm. Cut two channels each with a distance from the end of the wood of 8.3cm. The channel should be 4.4cm wide and 2.2cm deep. If you have a slightly different cross section of wood, ensure the cut is at the 8.3cm mark and the channel is the width of the wood you are using. Make four of these pieces.

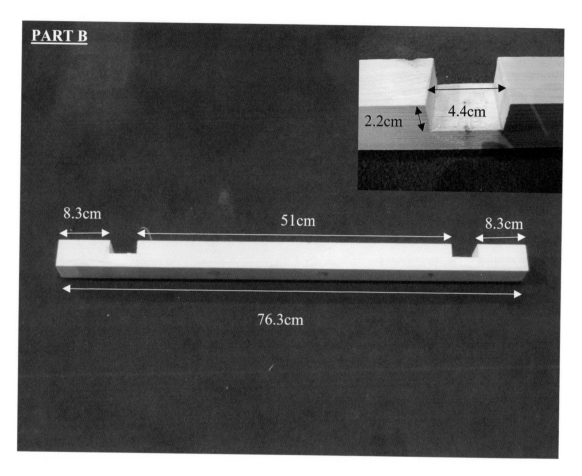

Select two of these pieces made above and turn them over such that the channels face the ground. You need to make 3 x 12cm diameter holes to a depth of 2.5cm as shown below. Make 2 of these:

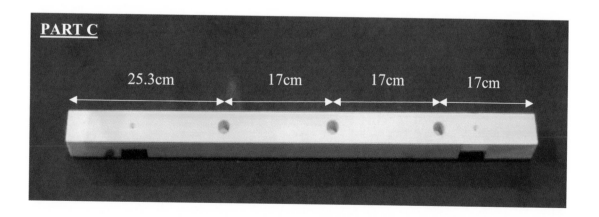

Cut a third length of wood 4.3cm² to a length of 65.7cm. Cut two channels each with a distance from the end of the wood of 4.4cm and 2.2cm deep. If you have a slightly different cross section of wood, make the width of your channel the width of your wood. Make two of these pieces.

PART D

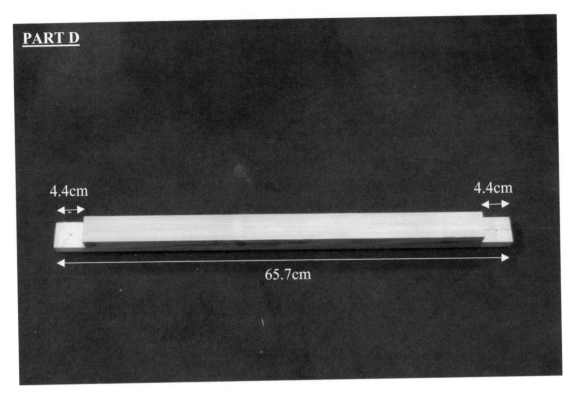

4.4cm   4.4cm

65.7cm

We are now going to assemble the side frames. Layout for the left and right-hand side frame are shown below:

LEFT SIDE FRAME – IMPORTANT: **Note the position and orientation of the wood with the 3 x 12cm holes (PART C)**

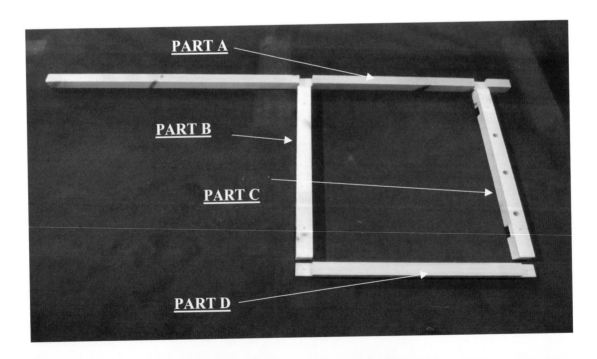

PART A

PART B

PART C

PART D

Once you have got the layout above, proceed to apply wood glue to the three faces in each of the channels and secure with 2 x 3cm wood screws on each channel joint. It should look as follows:

RIGHT SIDE FRAME – IMPORTANT: **Note the position and orientation of the wood with the 3 x 12cm holes (PART C).**

Note that the left and right-hand side frames are mirror images of each other. On the picture below, you can see the positioning of the hinges which will be dealt with in more detail below.

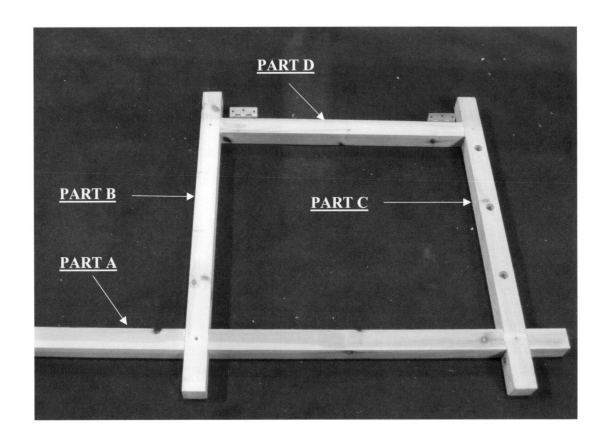

FRONT FRAME OF THEATRE

The front frame consists of 2 x Cross Bars, 2 x Uprights, a Plinth and a Header Board. These will be explained below:

CROSS BARS:

Cut a length of wood 4.3cm² to a length of 153.3cm. Cut two channels each with a distance from the end of the wood of 8cm. The channel should be 4.4cm wide and 2.2cm deep. If you have a slightly different cross section of wood, ensure the cut is at the 8cm mark and the channel is the width of the wood you are using. Make two of these pieces.

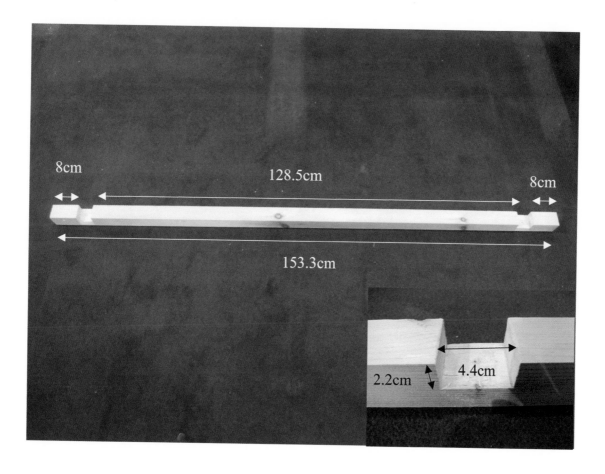

UPRIGHTS:

Cut a length of wood 4.3cm² to a length of 167cm. Cut two channels; one with a distance of 8cm from the end of the wood and one with a distance of 84cm from the other end of the wood. The channel should be 4.4cm wide and 2.2cm deep. If you have a slightly different cross section of wood, ensure the cut is at the 8cm and 84cm mark and the channel is the width of the wood you are using. Make two of these pieces.

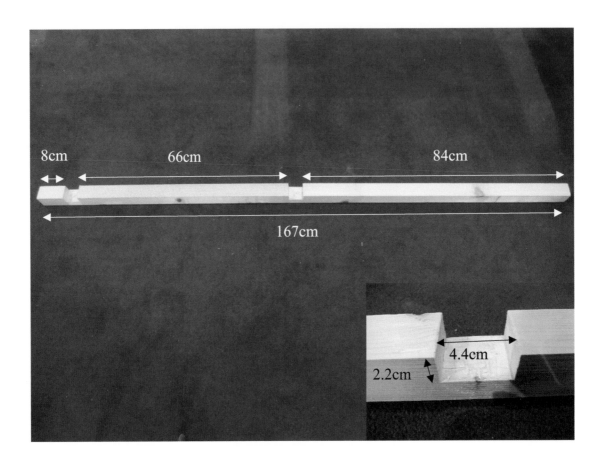

Plinth:

The plinth should be made from a single piece of pine of not less than 1.3cm thickness. The width should be 14cm and the length of 127cm. The plinth should be finely sanded and varnished as the plinth is where the children run their hands for the puppets.

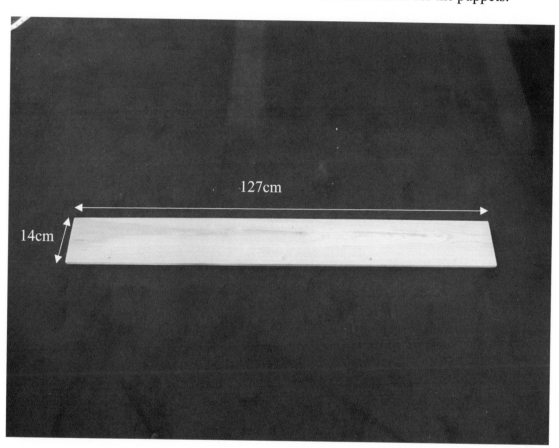

HEADER BOARD:

The header board should be made of 9mm plywood. The design of this and how it is painted are entirely up to you but the example below can be used as a template for any design you wish. Just a word of caution not to make it too tall as the overall height may cause issues going through doorways. It is best to cut plywood with a fine toothed electric jigsaw as this minimizes the splintering. Once you are happy with your Header Board outline, ensure it is fine sanded to eliminate splinters. The board can then be painted with primer and then a design in top coat paint applied.

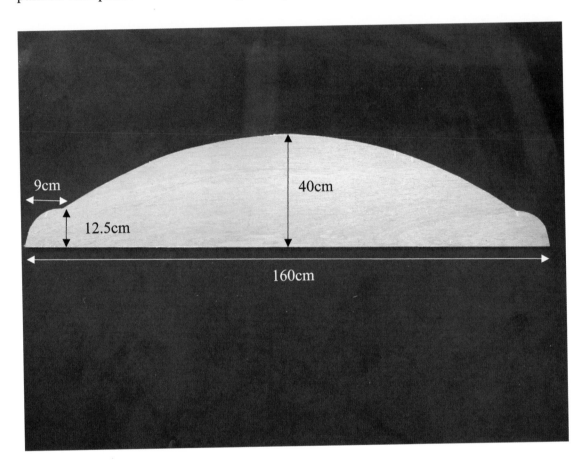

ASSEMBLY OF THE FRONT FRAME:

Layout the Cross Bars and Uprights as shown:

Preassemble without glue to ensure fit of all parts and make adjustments as necessary:

Disassemble the frame and apply wood glue to each of the channels' three faces cut in the Cross Bars. Reassemble and hold each joint firm by using 2 x 3cm wood screws.

Affix the Header Board to the top of the Front Frame using 3cm screws at 15cm intervals screwed first through the Header Board then into the wood of the frame.

Fix the plinth to the lower Cross Bar equidistant from the Uprights. Use 4cm screws at 15cm intervals as shown.

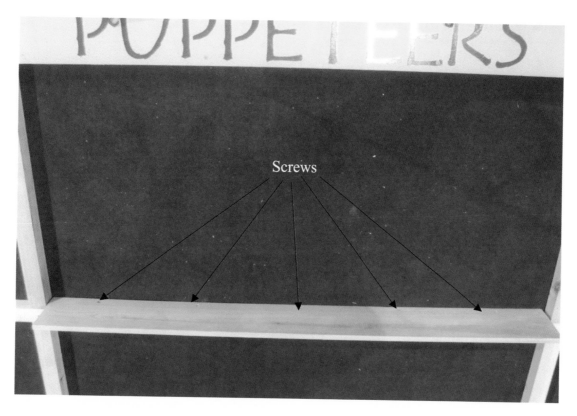

Your Front Frame should look like the picture below:

ASSEMBLY OF FRONT FRAME TO SIDE FRAMES

Turn the Front Frame over so that the facing side is resting on the floor. Then place the left Side Frame and right Side Frame into position as shown:

2 hinges should be attached between each Side Frame and the Front Frame. Below are some details on attaching the hinges.

ENSURE CLEARANCE BETWEEN
FRONT FRAME AND SIDE FRAME
WHEN OPENING SIDE FRAME

2cm

HINGES SHOULD BE SET BACK 2CM TOP
AND BOTTOM AS SHOWN

DOWELING AND BACK DROPS:

You need 3 lengths of 1cm diameter wooden dowel rod. It is best to cut these to length once the frame of the puppet theatre is completed. The dowel should be easily inserted, stable once in place and easily removable (for change of scenery by changing the backdrop). The lengths of the dowel below should therefore only be used as a rough guide.

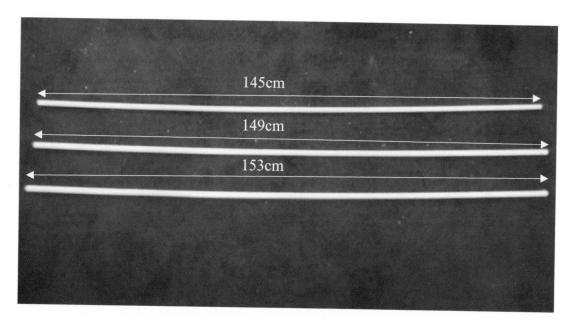

And here you can see the dowel rods inserted into the 12cm holes made in the top of the Side Frame (Part C). You can also see the way in which the Backdrop is sewn to allow the dowel to pass through it.

BACKDROPS

The Backdrops can be painted directly onto calico using a suitable material paint. Note that the calico should be folded over at the top and sewn so that the dowel rods can pass through and the Backdrop be suspended from it. Here are some examples:

Below you can see how the Theatre Frame with inserted Backdrops should look:

CURTAINING LOWER FRONT FRAME:

Using a piece of material of high thickness (or weight), turn over or hem the edges to makes a piece 200cm x 100cm. This will be stapled to the lower Front Frame of the theatre.

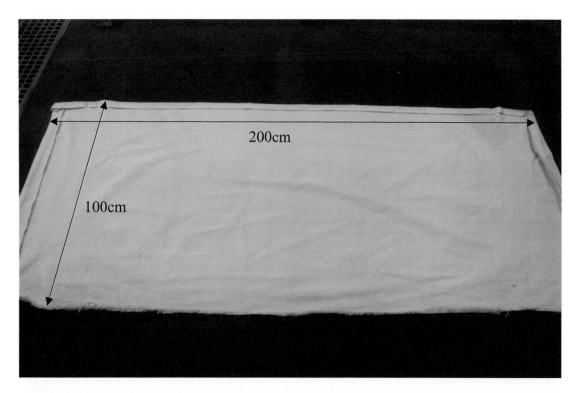

Centralise the material to the front frame. Using a power stapler, fix the material to the lower Crossbar (beneath the plinth) on the Front Frame as shown in the photo below:

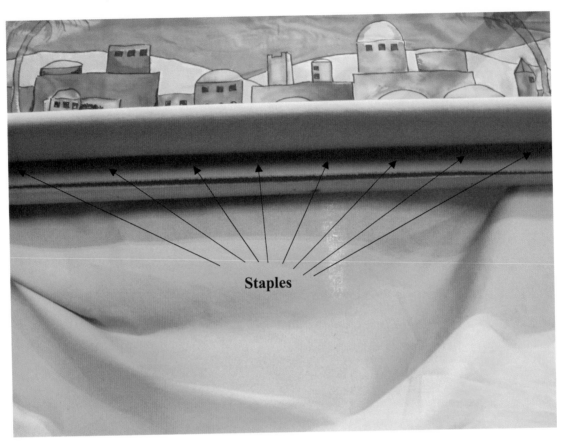

Secure the material to the ends of the lower Front Frame Crossbar as shown with three staples.

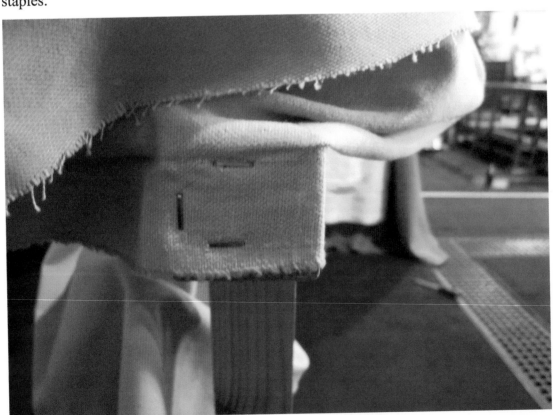

Secure the material to the back of the lower front frame Crossbar and Upright as shown.

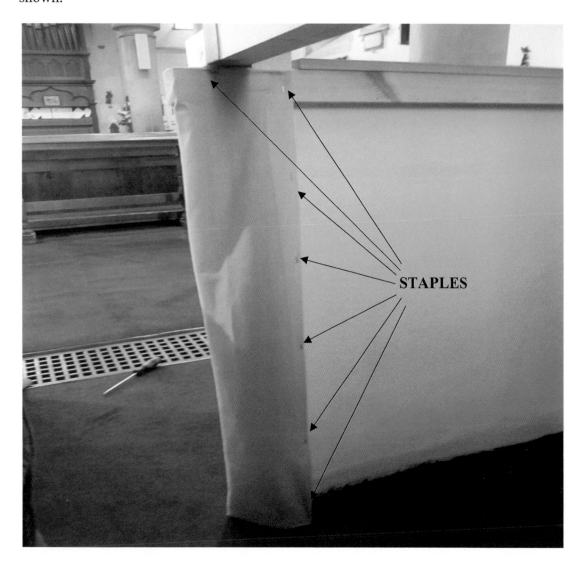

STAPLES

Repeat the stapling of the cloth to the Front Frame Upright on the other side and will complete the curtaining of the bottom of the Front Frame as shown.

LOWER SIDE FRAME CURTAINING

Cut two pieces of material (the same as the front panel), turn over or hem the edges to a size of 100cm x 142cm. These will be used to curtain the lower Side Frames

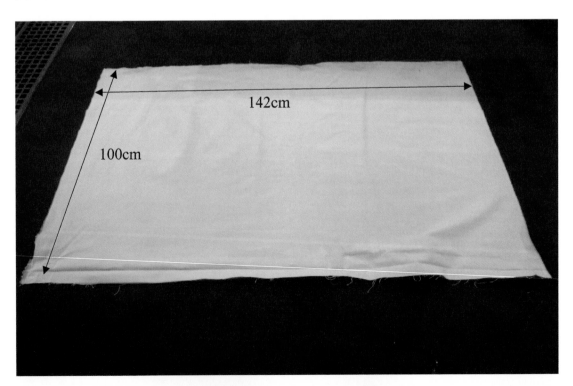

Staple the top of the curtain to the Side Frame – PART B

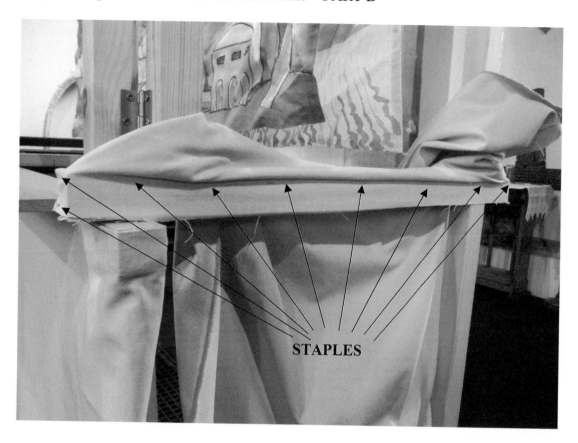

STAPLES

Then fold over the material to cover the Lower Side Frame

Bring the material around to the inside of the Side Frame and staple in the same way as above to Side Frame PART B:

Repeat this procedure to curtain the lower part of the opposite Side Frame – picture below:

UPPER SIDE FRAME CURTAINING

Cut two pieces of material (I used a light silky material), turn over or hem the edges to a size of 100cm x 150cm. These will be used to curtain the upper Side Frames.

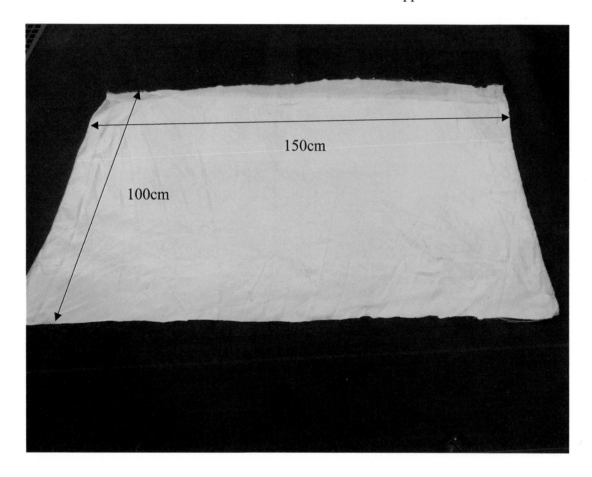

IMPORTANT: When fixing curtaining the upper Side Frames, ensure the Side Frame is flat against the Front Frame. Failure to do this will result in the material tearing when the Puppet Theatre is opened and free standing.

Staple the material to the Uprights on the Front Frame in the positions shown (i.e. between upper and lower Crossbars) then fold the material back on itself to hide the staples, resulting in the below:

At the base of the Upright next to the Plinth, fix staples in the positions shown:

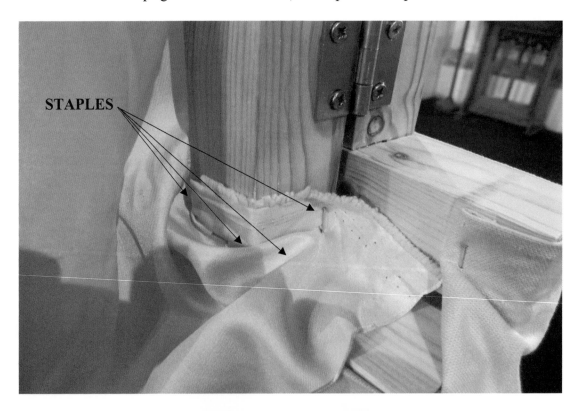

Insert a staple at the top of the Upright on the Front Panel.

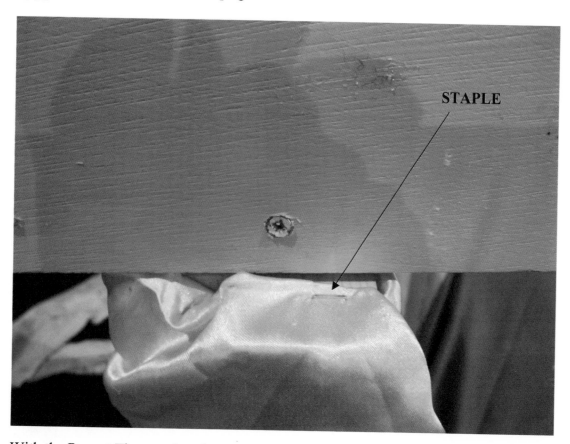

With the Puppet Theatre closed, wrap the material around PART D of the Side Frame and staple as shown below:

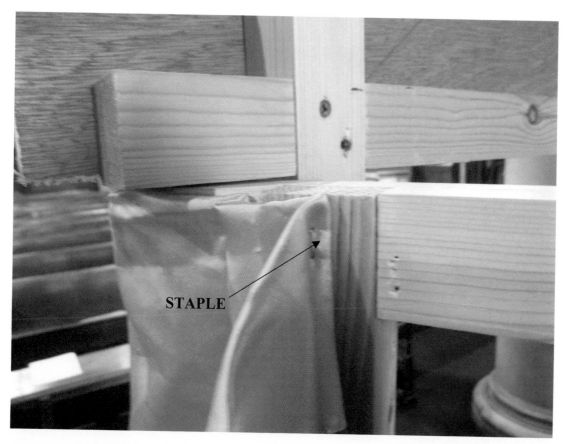

You then need to form a series of pleats at the top of the curtain securing each pleat in place with a staple. Once the first staple is in place, fold the material over the top of the Side Frame and continue forming pleats with staples at about 5cm intervals:

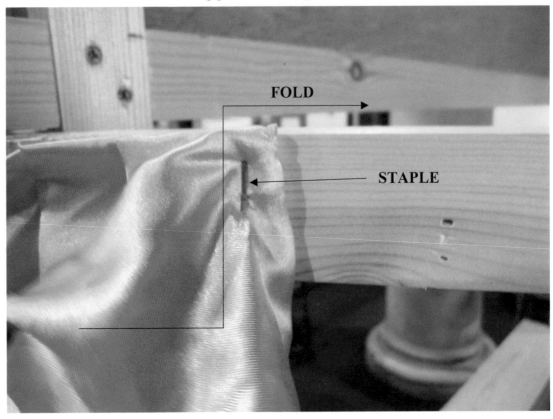

Below you can see a stapled and pleated top of Side Frame

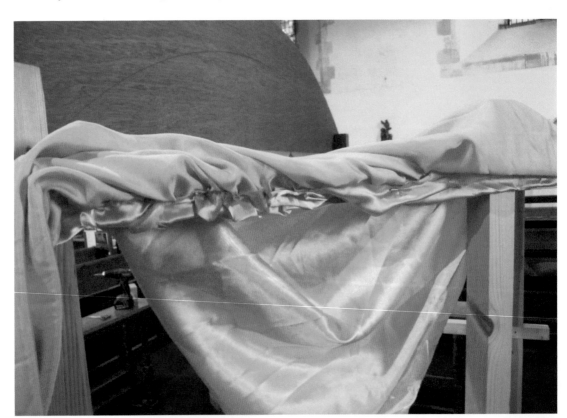

Allow the curtain to drop back – it should look as follows:

Then staple the Top Curtain on to the Side Frame Part B as shown below.

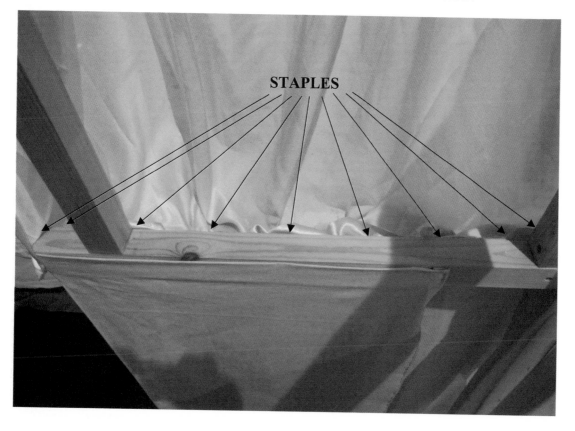

Repeat the above process to curtain the other Upper Side Frame

BELOW you can see the final assembled Puppet Theatre with the backdrop in place.

The Puppet Theatre can then be stored upright a flat against a wall, when the dowels and Backdrops are removed. Store the Backdrops in a dry place and ensure the Puppet Theatre is secure against the wall so that it cannot fall on children who may be tempted to play with it.

Old Testament - The Chosen One

Resources:

Puppet theatre
4 male puppets
Priest to speak the words of "Lord" outside the puppet theatre.

Background:

This play centres on the anointing of David (son of Jesse) by Samuel who in turn received his instruction from the Lord.

....

Narrator:

And The Lord said to Samuel.

Lord:

Get some olive oil and go to Bethlehem.

Samuel:

Are we going to do some cooking?

Lord:

Nooooo. We are going to see a man called Jesse because one of his sons will be king and we will be anointing him.

Samuel:

I would prefer to do some cooking.

Lord: {shouts}

Do as I command!

Narrator:

Samuel did as the Lord commanded and went to Bethlehem. He found Jesse and asked him to present his sons to him so that Samuel, inspired by the Lord, could tell Jesse which of his sons would be king.

Samuel:

Jesse, one of your sons will be a king.

Jesse:

What, King of the awkward squad? They drive me mad you know – nothing I ever do is right. Until they are twelve, you are the fount of all knowledge, now I know nothing apparently.

Samuel:

A good job I will be telling them then. Look Jesse, one of your sons will be king; the Lord our God has told me and will work through me to tell you which is the chosen one. Are you game or not?

Jesse:

Very well. Let the contest begin! Contestant number one, come forward!

Son 1:

I am six feet tall, handsome with a distinctive beard, can play the bagpipes and enjoy modern art.

Lord:

Pay no attention to how tall and handsome he is. I reject him because I do not judge as men and women judge but I look at the heart (also those bagpipes didn't help).

Narrator:

Then Jesse called his second son and brought him to Samuel.

Jesse:

Contestant number two, come forward. You may be a king but Samuel has to assess you first.

Son 2: {stroppy}

Do I have to?

Jesse:

Yes.

Son 2: {sulky}

OK, here I am, can I go now?

Samuel:

Please do!

Jesse:

Contestant number three, up you come.

Samuel:

No

Jesse:

Contestant number four!

Samuel:

Definitely no.

Jesse:

Contestant number five.

Samuel:

No again.

Jesse:

Contestant number six, your turn!

Samuel:

The Lord does not choose him either strangely. Do you have any more sons that we can speak to?

Jesse:

I have my youngest Son, David, but he is out looking after the sheep. Actually, I really hope he is looking after the sheep otherwise I am going to have a very sleepless night. Counting camels never does it for me.

Samuel:

Tell him to come here. We won't offer the sacrifice until he comes.

Narrator:

Jesse sent for David. He was handsome and healthy and didn't play the bagpipes.

The Lord:

This is the one. Anoint him!

Narrator:

Samuel took the olive oil and anointed David in front of his brothers. Immediately, the spirit of the Lord took control of David and was with him from that day on and he became King David. THE END.

Christmas – Three Wise Men and a Camel

Resources:

Puppet theatre
5 male puppets

Background:

This play puts a lighter perspective on the Magi visiting evil King Herod. Where indicated the words can be sung or said – various tunes will work but Three Little Birds works quite well or they can speak it. When the Holy Spirit sings you could have all the children singing. Herod is portrayed as liking his food a bit too much. The Narrator could be played by the Camel puppet.

....

Narrator:

I'm back for the play you've been waiting for all year. The children's Christmas play. *{Cheers}* Our story this year is a subtle blend between the Charles Dickens book " A Christmas Carol" and the story of Christmas. Try to stay awake and follow along this time _____ *{name someone suitable in the congregation who can take a joke}* . Jesus will be Tiny Tim, Herod will be Scrooge, Bob Marley will be the Holy Spirit, God will be the Ghosts of past, present and future and Mary and Joseph will be Tiny Tim's parents. I told you to keep awake! And here we go!!

Herod:

Baaa Humbug. ------ Trebor Mint, ----- Liquorice Allsort. I do struggle to pick off the menu. Now where was I, oh yes that little birdie told me that Jesus is to be King of The Jews - I'll soon fix that. What do they think I am - made of gingerbread. Have we got any more pasties? – I'm starving.

Narrator:

Herod went to bed that night, having a rather strange dream. A Liquorice Allsort started chasing a Trebor Mint down the street; it caught it and painted it with black stripes which was then eaten by a giant sheep called Eric. Then he awoke.

Herod:

Baaaaa --- Humbug.

Narrator:

A vision appeared in front of Herod.

Holy Spirit:♫

Now Herod, Do, do , do, do ; Mend your ways, Do, do , do, do, do
I am warning you - to lay off the boy. Do, do , do, do, do
Intent on some evil deeds, I can tell you, you will not succeed
Three Eastern Kings, upon your doorstep
Saying sweet things, of prophecies pure and wise
Truly - This one true King cannot be denied

Herod:

Please stop singing - Baaa - Humbug. Who on earth are you to tell me what to do!

Holy Spirit:

You will be visited twice more before this night is over. Repent and mend your ways ugly .

Narrator:

And with that the Holy Spirit disappeared.

Herod: {shouts}

And please - stop singing. I am in charge and I will not yield to this boy Jesus.

Narrator:

Then the doorbell rang {knocks with a clave}.

Herod:

Who can that be?

Three Kings:♫

We are three wise men, with prophecies pure and wise.
To give this message to you, hoo, hoo, hoo

Herod:{in the manner of an evil genius rubbing his hands together)

Come in, come in dear chaps. Now I also want to pay my respects to the baby Jesus.
Tell you what, when you've found him why not come back and tell me where he is then
I can pay my respects - Mwah, ha, ha

Narrator:

The wise men agreed but that evening the Holy Spirit made a second appearance

Holy Spirit:♫

Now Magi, Do, do , do, do ;   Your quest is true, Do, do , do, do, do
But Herod is, a bit of cad. Do, do , do, do, do
He's intent on evil deeds, to kill the boy that you seek
Three Eastern Kings, return not to Herod
Go the long way around, go somewhere you cannot be found
Truly - This one true King cannot be denied

Magi:{shouting}

Righto! But please STOP singing, please!

Narrator:

Time passed, the singing did <u>not</u> improve, but the Magi arrived at the Cratchits house in Bethlehem.

Joseph:

Not today thank you, rather busy! Come back tomorrow!

Magi:

We come bearing gifts.

Joseph:{grumpy}

Well unless you have a pair of earplugs in there, go away.

Magi:

We have come to pay our respects to Baby Jesus, the Messiah. We have gifts of Gold, Frankincense and Myrrh.

Joseph:{happy}

Well why didn't you say so. Come in dear chaps, come in. The more the merrier eh Mary?

Narrator:

And with that, the choirs of Heaven rang out to celebrate the birth of the new baby, Jesus Christ with a special guest appearance from you know who.

Holy Spirit: ♫

Now Magi, Do, do , do, do ;   Your quest is done, Do, do , do, do, do
You've found him there, in a bed of straw. Do, do , do, do, do
He is the Lord Jesus Christ, saviour of all mankind
Three Eastern Kings, you fooled old Herod
What a long way you've come
Through perils to see our Lords' son
Truly - This one true King cannot be denied

Narrator:

And that is the end of that part of the story – and the singing hopefully. THE END.

Christmas – Donkey

Resources:
Puppet theatre
Puppets: A donkey and female puppet for Mary

Background:
Everyone knows people cannot understand what donkeys say and think. In this play, we get to hear some of the donkey's thoughts whilst Mary prepares to go to Bethlehem. This play is more fun if Mary has a posh accent! The song at the end is to the tune of Little Donkey.

....

Mary:
Little Donkey, will you carry me to Bethlehem? We have a very long way to travel and one does not think that one can walk that far. I am <u>so</u> tired what with the baby, the mood swings and the cravings. They take everything out of one. Will you carry me to Bethlehem?

Donkey:
Little Donkey - the clue is in the name. Little! Do I have a choice? I vote for lying down? Does anyone have a set of wheels?

Mary:
I can't imagine how tiring I'm going to find this journey, I'm so grateful Little Donkey.

Donkey:
You! you are going to find this tiring! Saints preserve us. Call me your shrunken beast of burden. Not sure how that will work in the songs to come.

Mary:
You are <u>so</u> un-suffering on my account with hardly a word of complaint. Let me just mount up here.

Donkey:
OOF…. no one said about carrying two persons. This is a single carriage vehicle with no tandem capability. Any chance of a diet before we head off? *{Pause}*
I'll take that as a no.

Mary:
Little donkey, see the long road ahead we will need all our resilience and strength to make it to Bethlehem on time for the census.

Donkey: {he is struggling with the load}

OOF, OOOFF you aren't kidding. Why couldn't I have been born a horse or, or, or how about a camel, 3x the power, twice as high off the ground and all you can drink for a week. It isn't natural to sit on a beast of burden such that "ones" sandals scrape the ground.

Mary:

At last little donkey, we have arrived and our prayers have been answered.

Donkey:

Only - when - you - dismount (grunting).

Mary:

The journey was long and dangerous....

Donkey:

Only for my back Mary; only for my back!

Mary:

And this difficult trip will be remembered for ever after when the lord Jesus is born.

Donkey:

And in 2000 Years - I hope they remember the poor soul that did the carrying and he gets a song all to himself. I hope they sing of me

(To the tune of Little Donkey)
Powerful steed, oh wonderful donkey
Under a tremendous load.
Da da dah da, dad a dah da, dah dad ah dah dah

Mary:

I didn't know Donkeys could sing!

Donkey:

You have a cutting sense of humour Mary. And that my dear friends is the end of our short play describing the real journey to Bethlehem. THE END.

Christmas
I'm An Animal - and I Can Get you Out of Here!!

Resources:

Puppet theatre
Puppets:
Some animal puppets (donkey, elephant, squirrel, mouse, camel)
1 x female puppet
1 x male puppet
1 x Grandpa puppet

Background:

Why did Mary choose a donkey to take her to Bethlehem? Maybe it was because a donkey or maybe he won a contest! Unlikely I know but let's go with it shall we?

. . . .

Mary:

I had to go to Bethlehem to register for the census. I wondered how on earth I was going to walk there while carrying Gods son. I thought some transport was in order. In fact, the choice was limited - so let's go back in time and you will see that fiction is indeed stranger than the facts.

Time travel: Dr Who Music

TV Presenter: {ham it up!!}

So welcome too..... " I'm an Animal and I can Get You Out of Here." The reality show that is as exciting as Waterskiing in the Everglades. *(Pause)* Now for those of you who don't know the rules, we have a Golden Buzzer which lets anyone with a compelling case go through to the final.

This week ladies and gentlemen we have 4 willing volunteers. We have
      Camel - from Surbiton, *{applause}*
      Giant Squirrel - from the Forest of Dean *{applause}*
      Elephant - from Eccles *{applause}*
      and Donkey - from Dartford *{applause}*
      and a late contestant who appears to be a bit lost. And who are you Sir?

Grandpa:

Is this the 18-30 Club?

TV Presenter:

No - Go Away. Now Camel - the congregation would like to know what makes you ideal transport for Mary.

Camel: {haughty}

I have long legs which means I am fast. I will not need to stop for water so you will have a quicker journey. I can carry 2 people (Mary and Joseph). And I am a higher class of animal than this the hoi-polloi hereabouts. *{Spit} {Spit} {Spit}*.

TV Presenter:

Obviously - moving on, I am almost afraid to ask but Donkey what makes you the best qualified to carry Mary?

Donkey: {show boating}

Hi!
I'm Donkey - suave in a glass! I'm the Best *{flicks head}* - no reason, just the Best *{flicks head}*. No need to boast but I am *{flicks head}* slow but sure. It might take a few months but *{flicks head}* I will be more comfortable than Stupid Squirrel! Hah - see what I did there?
I A-lliterated - Hah.

TV Presenter:

Well if Mary wants to be sick we have a winner. Giant Squirrel, what makes you an ideal transport for Mary?

Squirrel:

You should pick me because I'm good at running so I could get you there really, really quickly and avoid danger better than the others by running up trees. But you would have to wait for me to get my nuts first and then I am better than Dumb Donkey. Hah see what I did there?
I got him back - with I - lliteration.

TV Presenter:

And lastly Elephant, why would you be the best transport for Mary?

Elephant:

Well - I could sit on bandits. Free water available from my trunk. Bigger is always better but I need to let you know I have a medical condition - Mouseophobia

TV Presenter: What?

Elephant:

Fear of mice - nothing else, just mice. I go to bits you see.

{Mouse crosses puppet theatre}

Elephant:

{Screams and sits on Grandpa who is still lost}

Mary:

{Presses Golden Buzzer}
I think it should be Donkey - for entertainment value alone.

Donkey:

I thank you! *{to the audience}*! Also available for Parties, Baptisms and Bar Mitzvah's.

Mary:

Camel - sorry but the Son of God has standards you know - spitting - filthy habit.
Elephant - one mouse and I would fear for our safety.
Squirrel - sorry but the Son of God cannot wait for you to find your nuts.
THE END.

Christmas
Three Kings, One Camel:

Resources:
Puppet theatre
Puppets:
Donkey, Camel,
3 Male Puppets

Background:
Let's join the three wise men before their journey to Bethlehem and eve's drop on their conversations. The song at the end is to the tune of "We Three Kings".

....

Donkey:
This is a play about the 3 wise men and their journey on their camel to see the baby Jesus in Bethlehem. I volunteered to play the camel but they went and bought a new puppet.

King 1:
I am having a crisis of identity – some say I am a wise man and some say I am a king. Now look at me - good clothes, clever, handsome - I could be a King but I haven't got any land so I must be a Wise Man.

King 2:
Well wise man, what do you want to do that's wise?

King 3:
Please don't ask him that, you know it will be complete garbage what he comes up with.

King 1:
I have it – I am going to say something - Very profound.

King 3:
Take Cover – here it comes!

King 1:
Let's follow that big bright star in the sky.

King 2:
Pure genius – did you come up with that all by yourself?

King 1:
Actually I did!

King 3:

Are you sure you don't want to go to the moon or scale the North Face of Everest – something more worthwhile?

King 1:

I haven't told you the best part yet.

King 3:

Second volley – incoming!

King 1:

We will find a new born baby at the end of it!

King 3:

I think you are thinking of gooseberry bushes.

King 1:

The Son of God is not to be found under a gooseberry bush – he will be in a stable.

King 3:

That makes a big difference does it?

King 2:

And when shall we need to leave to be able to get there on time?

King 1:

Slight problem there – he has been born.

King 2:

You really are a genius – you know that!

King 1:

And we will need to find some transport and we can sing fine songs on the way to keep up our spirits on the treacherous journey. We need a ship for speed.

King 3:

We are surrounded by dessert

King 1:

Then we need a ship of the dessert – a camel or a dune buggy.

Camel: {Australian Accent – slowly}

G'day sport. Did someone call for a ship of the dessert. Here I am. 31 careful owners- 12 mad, 3 blind, 4 died of heat exhaustion, 5 trampled, one sat on a snake (sadly no longer with us), 4 fell off on the way, and 3 made it in one piece. 50 gold coins if I get you there – 25 if I don't

King 1:

Perfect – we'll take you. Do you know any dune buggies?

Camel:

No. Now maths was never my strong point but you are 3 and I am 1.

King 1:

OK - we'll take turns. Let's go!

Donkey:

So the three wise men set off on their journey to find the baby Jesus. Now many songs are sung of their journey with the most famous sung at Christmas every year. However whilst the tune was right, the words got changed over time – let's eavesdrop on the original.

King 2:

Now in my spare time on this camel I have written a song to keep us going – can we sing it?

King 1:

Sure –

All Kings and Camel:

♫We three Wise Men follow a star
Wish we were able to go in the car
We're tired, we're hungry the camel is bumpy
Wish we were sat at a bar
Ohh OHHH
Why did we set off so late
We're going to see the baby – great!
Westward heading, nowt for bedding
So much for the 3 wise men

King 1:

I get the feeling you are still not 100% sold on this holy quest.

King 2:

You think!

Donkey:

And much later than expected, the 3 wise men arrive at Bethlehem with their camel, tired hungry and most of all very thirsty but very happy to find the baby Jesus. THE END.

Christmas
We Brought What?

Resources:

Puppet theatre
Puppets:
Donkey,
3 Male Puppets

Background:

Imagine the 3 Kings trying to decide which gifts to present to the Lord Jesus Christ knowing he was only a baby and knowing they were part of the most significant story on earth. Let's sneak a look on they made the decision. The song at the end is to the tune of The Little Drummer Boy.

....

Narrator:

The Three Wise Men or is it Three Kings of Orient or is it the Magi. We are a bit unclear on what their title was. Actually, we are a little bit early I know for epiphany. But then as well as being dodgy on timing, we are also a bit dodgy on the number of Kings. But at least we all know what the gifts were and there was no confusion there --- or ---was there?

King 1: {officious voice}

Mary and Joseph, we are 3 Kings and we bring gifts appropriate for the Son of God for that was what we derived from our studies of the firmament. See, we have brought gold – fit for a King; Frankincense, a rare and expensive extract of tree gum for burning and producing a heavenly aroma. And - Myrrh??

King 2:

What did he say?

King 3:

Myrrh.

King 2:

No. Please No. We travelled 1000 miles through bandit country with extreme hardship to bring him - myrrh. Myrrh - a prefiguring of death and embalming - for the Son of God - for the baby Jesus who one day, will defy death and be resurrected.
We all saw it - death and resurrection. It's why we're here!!
Myrrh - can he get nothing right?

Narrator:

Impossible as it is to believe, I to have dropped some clangers in my time - but I think that takes the biscuit. Through the magic of the Puppeteers, let's go back a few years to work out how they ended up with the gifts that they brought and managed to drop the clanger of all clangers.

King 2:

Okay, we all interpreted the signs the same way did we not brothers. We the 3 most brilliant…

King 1:

..and modest…

King 2:

minds of our time, know that the most important person in the world, now or ever, will be born as the Son of God. We know where. We know when. We, as the cream of the intelligentsia must travel and welcome him into this world. We run great risks and hardship on this immense journey; we leave our families and all comfort behind. Are we agreed?

King 1:

Biscuits! – you said there'd biscuits for this meeting. Everyone knows you can't make headway on important issues when you are thinking about food.

King 3:

This is important - forget the biscuits! We need to contemplate and cogitate about the gifts we will take. We have an important decision to make and we must leave soon.

King 1:

Easy, it's a baby – take some baby toys. He won't care what they are - he'll just suck them anyway.

King 3:

Baby toys – for the Son of God? Really! I think you're trivializing the significance of this momentous occasion.

King 1:

Okay – how about this - a magic sheep?

King 2:

A brilliant idea with only two issues! Firstly, they don't exist and secondly if they did, it would magic itself away from your stupidity at the first opportunity. Can we have ideas for gifts that actually exist.

King 2:

Money. We could take some money – very useful is money. Gives you options and opportunities.

King 1:

That's fine but when they he gets older, he'll spend it on sweets. I did!

King 3:

We'll give it to his parents then; they can put it in the Bank of Bethlehem for him until he's older.

King 2:

Rather than money, let's take gold.

King 1&3:

Agreed!

King 1:

You know that stable's gonna stink. Where you have cows and sheep you have -the unpleasant side as well. You know - the other end.
Did you know a dairy cow produces 400 litres of methane a day?

King 3:

A no smoking sign would be in order then!

King 1:

Be serious. Something to perfume the air. Something like Frankincense. Expensive, spiritual, holy and sweet smelling. Practical and appropriate.

King 3 and 2:

Agreed!

King 3:

How about some reading material?

King 2:

He can't read!

King 3:

The Son of God can't read! There's hope for me yet! What about a Donkey – transportation for the journey home.

King 2:

Have you met Donkey? They would never get a moments peace and it would keep the baby awake with all its jabbering.

Donkey:

Charming! I'll be on next year folks.

King 1:

Please go and get the biscuits and do something useful.

King 3:

I thought you'd never ask.

King 2:

Now it gets pretty chilly at night in the desert. I know they are in a stable and get animal warmth but they will have to go home at some point and on their homeward journey, the night will be cold. I was thinking maybe some animal skins to keep him warm.

King 1:

Capital idea. Oh, here are the biscuits.

King 2:

OK, we're that's it. We will take Gold, Frankincense and Fur as gifts for the baby Jesus. Are you listening to me King 3?

King 3:

Mmmmpphh (spits biscuit).

Narrator:

Ahhhhh. I see the issue.
So, the moral to that story is always serve good biscuits <u>prior</u> to an important meeting or the consequences could be severe. Oh, and hang on, the 3 Kings are Singing their Lullaby to the baby Jesus.

All: ♫:

Come they told us pa, ra, pum, pum, pum
A newborn King to see pa, ra, pum, pum, pum
Our finest gifts we bring pa, ra, pum, pum, pum
To lay before the King pa, ra, pum, pum, pum
Ra, pum, pum, pum, Ra, pum, pum, pum
We came many miles pa, ra, pum, pum, pum

King 1:

Many miles

King 3:

Furs, they told me pa, ra, pum, pum, pum

All:

Gold and some Frankincense pa, ra, pum, pum, pum

King 2:

Our finest gifts we thought pa, ra, pum, pum, pum

All:

To lay before the King pa, ra, pum, pum, pum
Ra, pum, pum, pum, Ra, pum, pum, pum

All:

We had one deaf plank pa, ra, pum, pum, pum

King 3:

And we tanked

King 2:

Fur was then misheard pa, ra, pum, pum, pum

King 3:

I heard the fur as myrrh pa, ra, pum, pum, pum
I just felt so absurd pa, ra, pum, pum, pum
Could have been lemon curd pa, ra, pum, pum, pum
Ra, pum, pum, pum, Ra, pum, pum, pum
Then he smiled at me pa, ra, pum, pum, pum
The Lord has come!

THE END.

Easter – Roman Soldiers

Resources:

Puppet theatre
2 male puppets
1 female puppet

Background:

What do you think two ordinary Roman soldiers would have made of the events when Jesus was resurrected. Perhaps they were passive observes to the strange goings on at the time. What if they were interviewed? In this play one soldier is brighter than the other but both would struggle to find the head on a hammer much to the frustration of the interviewer – if they had TV back then, of course. Get the kids playing the soldiers to shout "Sah" or "Mam" every time it comes up – they think it's great fun. Have the Priest be the narrator to introduce this. By the way, some of the words are written phonetically to get the personalities across so give the kids help on this.

....

Narrator:

And now we go over to our Ace Reporter Fiona Spruce.

Fiona:

Thank you narrator. I am in Jerusalem standing near the scene of the mysterious disappearance of the boy made good from Nazareth. I speak of none other than Jesus Christ himself. I have managed to find some witnesses who are willing to speak to us so let me bring them in now.

Now you are both soldiers serving in the Roman army, and you are both looking a little nervy if I may say so. Soldier….

Soldier 1:

Sah! – – - - - I mean Mam.

Fiona:

What has been going on here?

Soldier 1:

Mostly we is bin standin - mam!

Fiona:

Resurrection??

Soldier 1:

Nope – I'm still alive – thanks – Mam!

Fiona: {getting frustrated}
Not for much longer!! Jesus <u>Christ's</u> resurrection?

Soldier 2:
She means the man on the Cross where all the weird stuff happened.

Soldier 1:
Mam – right mam. Yep. Amazin – has me at a loss Sah - Mam!!

Fiona:{to the congregation}
I could have been a nurse you know but OOhh no, I have to interview the cream of the Roman army. I'd have more luck with Donald Duck – if he'd been invented.

Soldier 2:
I'd have been a dentist but a draft came through.

Soldier 1:
It does gets draughty in this armour if you know what I mean.

Soldier 2:
I meant compulsory call up into the army.

Fiona: {more frustrated}
Please – I beg you. Stop prattling and answer some simple questions.

Soldiers 1 &2:
Sah – Mam (together)

Soldier 2:
It all started when Jesus was brought before the Roman Governor, Pontius Pilate.

Fiona:
Who eventually condemned Jesus to death of course. What was your involvement here?

Soldier 1:
Mostly standin – Mam!

Soldier 2:
Let me translate - we had to guard him. We went all the way to the hill outside the city with him. Some of the more senior soldiers divided his possessions between them, and we had to stay until the prisoners died.

Fiona:
Not a nice job to have to do.

Soldier 1:
Toilets is worse Mam! Sah! Mam!

Soldier 2:
Agreed but only just. Jesus didn't blame us. He took his death quite calmly. It went completely dark even though it was the middle of the afternoon, then as he died there was an earthquake. It all felt very wrong. When Jesus died I found myself calling out that he really was the Son of God!

Fiona:
And what did you do soldier?

Soldier 1:
Came over funny and – well, fainted - then woke on impact Sah! Mam!

Soldier 2:
A little later orders came to take Jesus' body down from the cross. One of his followers offered us a tomb to put him in, so we let him take the body there. But we followed and the tomb was sealed with a huge stone

Soldier 1:
I bagsied the stone and sealed it Sah!

Fiona: {very angry now}
Mam! - Not Mam Sah Mam! Or Sah Mam. Just Mam – got it!

Soldier 1:
Sah! Mam!

Fiona: {resigned}
I am going to have a crisis in a minute – carry on

Soldier 2:
Well then, we took it in turns to keep watch over the tomb.

Fiona:
So were you there when the tomb was actually opened?

Soldier 1:
Sah! - We just come back on watch - nuffin 'appened all the time before. Then suddenly there was an earfquake! Sah!

Soldier 2:

At the same time an angel appeared in front of us – he just glowed white. He rolled the massive stone away, as if it didn't weigh anything at all!

Fiona:

So did you actually see Jesus walk out of the tomb?

Soldier 1:

Sah! Err no sah!….We wuz lying on the floor out stone cold! Shock and everyfin….

Fiona: {sarcastically}

I can see it must have been an incredible and highly challenging few days for you two.

Soldier 2:

It was the most important few days of my life. I mean Jesus <u>must</u> be the Son of God – earthquakes, angels and coming back to life! I think we will both be looking for Jesus now – to listen to his message.

Fiona:

Well there you have it folks - it looks like Jesus may have two new followers (heaven help him!) Roman soldiers off to listen to Jesus' message, whatever next?

Back to you in the church!

Easter – And Jesus Awoke

Resources:
Puppet theatre
2 male puppets

Background:
Two school friends are discussing the resurrection and trying to make sense of it all.
Look out for the Spock quote.

....

Narrator:
Good morning everyone. Have you ever really wondered what happened in that tomb
in which Jesus was laid after he had been crucified. Have you ever tried to make sense
of this story to the ascension? No – well, this is what the Sunday School came up with.
Maybe it is not what happened but there are some points in here that will make you
think more deeply over Easter – we hope!

Alex:
So Jesus was crucified on the cross, maybe he wasn't dead when they put him in the
tomb and that's how the tomb was empty. He recovered and walked out.

Arthur:
They put a spear in his side to make sure he was dead! I think that would stop him
from wandering around.

Alex:
I suppose he wouldn't have had the strength to move the stone from the inside
especially as it was sealed with a small stone to stop the big stone being rolled away.

Arthur:
It says here that two Angels were in the tomb. Why were there two angels? When
Mary was told she was going to have a baby and to name him Jesus, only the angel
Gabriel appeared to her. Also, there was only one angel that appeared to Joseph

Alex:
Well you must need two angels to roll back the stone

Arthur:
But Jesus was dead.

Alex:
In the bible it says that the angels asked Mary why she was looking among the dead for
one who is alive. Yes - Jesus was dead as we understand it. It was a tomb and he must
have walked out. But that doesn't answer how he turned into a gardener and spoke to
Mary and then turned back into Jesus so Mary could recognise him.

Arthur:

When Mary saw the Angels she saw Jesus in the gardener; she probably recognised his voice and mannerisms. Jesus was speaking through the gardener rather than Jesus turning into the gardener and back again.

Alex:

So the same thing happened when Jesus met the men on the road to Emmaus?

Arthur:

Not quite. The men on the road to Emmaus knew Jesus very well – they were followers so they would have recognised him. He must have looked like someone else like when he was speaking through the gardener. When they were having dinner and when he broke the bread he disappeared though. Maybe that was more like a very real ghost.

Alex:

But when he appeared to Thomas, he was flesh and blood Thomas was able to touch him.

Arthur:

And at that point, Jesus has a physical form like when he left the tomb but the story that defies any explanation is when he was taken up to heaven at Bethany. Who can raise his arms and be taken up to heaven.

Alex:

As the saying goes "Once you eliminate the impossible, whatever remains, no matter how improbable, must be the truth." It is impossible that Jesus was alive after being crucified yet many people physically saw the Jesus with the marks of his death and Jesus spoke to many people. Many people saw him taken up into heaven at Bethany as he was blessing them.

Arthur:

However improbable, it seems like the resurrection is the truth. THE END.

Easter – The Jerusalem Herald

Resources:
Puppet theatre
1 male puppet
1 female puppet

Background:
This play tells the story about Mary Magdalene discovering the empty tomb of Jesus. The narrator should be voiced by the Priest and see if he/she twigs the first gag.

....

Narrator:
And now we go over to our Ace reporter Benjamin Net and Yahoo

Benjamin:
Thank you narrator. I am in Jerusalem standing outside the scene of the mysterious disappearance of the boy made good from Nazareth. I speak of none other than Jesus Christ himself. I have managed to find a number of witnesses who are willing to speak to us so let me bring them in now.

Now you are Mary Magdalene, one of Jesus' most loyal supporters. Tell me Mary, what was it that happened here yesterday?

Mary:
Well – I was going to the tomb and when I approached I saw that the great heavy sealing stone had been rolled back. Now that stone would be impossible to move on your own and there were some Roman guards outside.

Benjamin:
So who moved it?

Mary:
Well truth be told, there was an earthquake earlier that day. At that moment everyone was completely terrified because an Angel appeared. We had never seen one before

Benjamin:
An angel – can you explain?

Mary:
It was the angel that rolled back the stone – that was what one of the guards said. Actually, the cream of the Roman army had turned tail and abandoned the tomb when that happened. An Angel also appeared to us. We were told to stay calm and not be afraid. Then the angel said that that Jesus had risen from the dead.

Benjamin:

Wow, amazing. So, what happened next? Earthquake, walking dead, I suppose you stayed where you were?

Mary:

Not at all, for some strange reason we were just excited; very excited. We ran all the way up there to see what was happening and who should we meet on the track but Jesus. It was definitely him, holes and everything!

Benjamin:

Incredible - what did you say to him?

Mary:

It wasn't so much what was said, more how I felt. I fell to my knees, I felt weak and speechless - which is **really** unusual for me! It was like being next to God – everything was very real.

Benjamin:

And did he say anything to you?

Mary:

Only that I should go to the disciples and tell them everything that had happened. Oh - and that they should meet him at Galilee.

Benjamin:

Well there you have it folks. Jesus has risen from the dead and is to be found somewhere near Galilee shortly.

Back to you in the church!

Easter – The Jerusalem Herald – Peter & John

Resources:
Puppet theatre
2 male puppets
1 female puppet

Background:
Imagine you could interview Peter and John at the time of Jesus' death and
resurrection. If you could speak to Peter and John, what would they tell you?
Something pretty amazing I am sure. Have the Priest be the narrator and have a
seamless segway into the play.

....

Narrator:
And now we go over to our Ace reporter Fiona Spruce. Come in Fiona.

Fiona:
Thank you narrator. I am in Jerusalem standing near the scene of the mysterious
disappearance of the boy made good from Nazareth. I speak of none other than Jesus
Christ himself. I have managed to find some witnesses who are willing (well I have
them cornered) to speak to us so let me bring them in now.

You are two of Jesus followers I believe, Peter and John - so things must have seemed
pretty bad last Friday?

Peter:
With the donkey eating a bad bag of oats?

John:
She means Jesus!

Peter:
Oh! - well it couldn't really get much worse, could it?

Fiona:
I realise that, but I'm just trying to get to how you were feeling?

Peter:
She's after that modern man approach - trousers - that sort of thing. Do we have to?

Fiona:
Yes - don't you want to be in print?

Peter:
I'd rather be in bed.

John:

Well - it all seemed unreal really. Looking back, Jesus had tried to warn us about what would happen, but we just hadn't understood.

Peter:

It was worse than anything we had imagined - though the donkey......

Fiona:

So what did you do with yourself over the next couple of days?

John:

Not a lot really

Peter:

Oh I wouldn't say that. We all hung around together getting really miserable.

Fiona:

So what changed things? You're not so miserable now!

Peter:

Certainly not Fiona! Bouncing off the walls is a more accurate description at the moment!

John:

And I thought it was the 72 chocolate eggs you ate.

Fiona:

So what happened?

Peter:

I felt a bit sick and...

Fiona:

About Jesus!

John:

Mary Magdalene came running, telling us that Jesus' body had been taken from the tomb. So, we ran there as fast as we could. I got there first - I'm a really good sprinter. I looked in and saw there was no body there.

Peter:

I caught up and went in the tomb and saw that Jesus' body had gone, but blow me down with a feather, only the linen cloths were left. And then I believed what he had told us, that he would rise from the dead.

Fiona:

So have you seen him?

John:

Not yet, but Mary Magdalene has, and we know that we will see him soon.

Fiona:

So you believe that, even though you haven't seen him yourself?

Peter:

Absolutely. Jesus is alive and we will see him soon. Life couldn't be better.

Fiona:

Well I will take your word for it, something has clearly cheered you up since Friday. 'Life couldn't be better', who would have thought it?

Back to you in the church!

Harvest Festival – It's a bit chilly up here

Resources:
Puppet theatre
3 puppets

Background:
For this play we go up to the artic and drop in on the conversation of 3 Inuit's. Not the usual setting for harvest festival but read on. The song is to the tune of Sing Hosanna.
....

Narrator:
For this Sunday School play we take you to the Arctic where the Inuit's live. We join three of the Inuit's sat in a circle hunting for fish through a hole in the ice.

Inuit 1:
Cccccccold isn't it. The only part of me that isn't cccccccold is my hair. Look I have an icicle on the end of my nose!

Inuit 2:
How is the farm going - anything sprouted yet?

Inuit 1:
Well I thought I saw something sprouting last week but then I remembered I had sneezed there the day before.

Inuit 2:
Nasty! Seriously?

Inuit 1:
Not really, no but it relieved the monotony for 2 minutes!! If I am really being hard on myself, the farm was probably a bad idea.

Inuit 2:
As ideas go, it's right up there with the specialist **ice cream shop** you opened last year.

Inuit 1:
Why do we live here anyway?

Inuit 3:
Fish, fish, fish and snow ball fights both of which get boring after the 10th day.

Inuit 1:
Don't forget the seals

Inuit 2:

Lovely. We have fish, snow and seals and we have to sit round this ice hole fishing for 10 hours a day. It's enough to drive you insane.

Inuit 3:

I like fishing

Inuit 1:

Good job really

Inuit 2:

Wouldn't it be nice to have something with the fish though. Anything in fact. I have heard that kids in the western world refuse to eat vegetables! Can you imagine, some nice green beans with the fish - wowzer!

Inuit 3:

Or some cauliflower or dare I say sprouts! Spuds would be something to try wouldn't they.

Inuit 1:

And some fruit to finish.

Inuit 2:

Oh stop it. You're making me hungry and you know we can't have them so why torment ourselves. Let's face it, if God had wanted us to eat veg, he would have made Inuit 1 open a grocery store! Let's sing something to keep our spirits up.

Inuit's - hit it!

All:

We love fish that is caught from the arctic,
But some veg would be oh so nice!
Eating taters or green stuff or pasta,
Or a lovely pile of hot French fries!

Chorus:
Fish with green beans, Fish with 'taters, Fish with carrots or with anything.
Fish with sweetcorn, Fish with cauli, fish with something God we pray.

Inuit 1:

I - have - a - bite lads!! Woo hoo - it feels like a whopper, this will feed us for a week.

Inuit 2:

Don't let it go, keep the line tight - here it comes. And we have - a basket of fruit? You don't see that every day in the Arctic now do you.
Inuit's take it away!

ALL:♫

We say thank you to God for the harvest,
All the fruit that we like to eat,
Lovely apples, bananas and grapefruit,
And the oranges that taste so sweet.

Chorus:
Thanks for 'nanas, thanks for grapefruits, thanks for apples we say thanks to God.
Thanks for oranges, thanks for lemons, thanks for fish and thank you God.

Inuit 2:

Guys, I got a bite as well. Something to go with the fruit. And here it comes, and I have - another basket of fruit! Yes Siree.

Inuit's, one more time

ALL:♫

Tomatoes are good in a fish pie,
And strawberries taste so fine.
We might even knock up a cob salad,
It's a shame there is no dry white wine!

Chorus
Sing tomatoes, sing tomatoes, sing tomatoes and say thanks to God.
Perfect strawberries, gorgeous blackberries, super melons thank you God.

Narrator:

Seven days later, Inuit 1 bought a local paper. The headline story was that a cargo ship had lost some of its load which happened to be washed under the ice sheet and perfectly preserved. God does indeed work in mysterious ways.

And that is the end of our play for Harvest - I bet you won't forget that one!

Harvest Festival – We Plough the Fields

Resources:
Puppet theatre
1 male puppet
1 female puppet

Background:
This is a good play for the kids to do at harvest and bringing the words of the old hymn "We Plough the Fields and Scatter" up to date. If you have a choir you can involve them or all the children can be the choir. Have fun
……………………………………………………………………………………………

Choir:♫
We plough the fields and scatter the good seed on the land.
But it is fed and watered by God's almighty hand.
He sends the snow in winter, the warmth to swell the grain.
The breezes and the sunshine and soft refreshing rain.
All good gifts around us are sent from heaven above.
So thank the Lord, oh thank the Lord, for all his love.

Wife:
What's all that racket about? Half of them are out of tune!

Man:
They're practicing my little wasps nest, for Harvest Festival, thanking God for all our food and so on.

Wife:
When did you last plough any fields? Or scatter any good seed? You sit and watch telly mostly but maybe, just maybe, after 30 minutes of intense nagging you scratch that bit of bare earth at the end of the lawn and chuck the seeds you have left over from last year!

Man:
Ah yes, however we do eat the marvelous bounty of my labour.

Choir:
We dig and rake the mud patch and throw seed on the ground…

Wife:
And you don't rely on the rain either – you use your hosepipe half the time.

Man:
Well not this year, with the hosepipe ban (hasn't this year been the wettest year on record?). Anyway, I wasn't breaking the ban!

Choir:♫
We dig and rake the mud patch and throw seed on the ground…
We water them with hosepipes, - unless there is a ban…

Wife:
And what about all those gro-bags you use from B and Q? That's not exactly natural, that's cheating that is!

Man:
But the tomatoes grow so much better in them, and I'm sure God doesn't mind - even if I do get them from B and Q.

Choir:♫
We dig and rake the mud patch and throw seed on the ground…
We water them with hosepipes, unless there is a ban.
The B and Q - grow-bags make my tomatoes swell…

Wife:
So you're saying that this still fits? It's completely different you lunatic! It's all about what you do – nothing to do with God.

Man:
Oh ye of little faith, my precious porcupine - not at all – if there is not enough rain, we must use our hosepipes but the water is still the water. And if the sun doesn't shine nothing grows as well. It's basic photosynthesis.

Wife:
You love the long words don't you!

Man:
It means a plant making food from air, water and sunlight - those are the gifts from our generous Lord. Without all 3 nothing grows.

Choir:♫
We dig and rake the mud patch and throw seed on the ground…
We water them with hosepipes, unless there is a ban.
The B and Q grow-bags make my tomatoes swell…
But if there is no sunlight they just don't do so well!

Man:
Here, did you know that a plant without light grows really tall to try and find light.

Wife:

Really!!! Don't you <u>ever</u> get tired?

Man:

No. It's called etiolation –

Wife:

You're very clever – deep – deep – deep – deep – deep – deep – deep – deep down.
And interesting! *{sarcastic}*

Man:

Yes I am.

Wife:

And modest.

Man:

Yes I am
Anyway what do you think of the new hymn?

Choir:♫

We dig and rake the mud patch and throw seed on the ground…
We water them with hosepipes unless there is a ban.
The Band Q grow-bags make my tomatoes swell…
But if there is no sunlight they just don't do so well!
We still need rain and sunshine sent by God above,
So thank the Lord, oh thank the Lord, for all his love.

Man:

THE END.

Harvest Festival – 1000 Ways to Kill a Brussel Sprout

Resources:
Puppet theatre
2 male puppets
2 female puppets

Background:
We all know kids hate sprouts (most do anyway). What if the Fairy God Farmer (FGF) were there – what would he do about it? Don't forget to give the FGF a broad Somerset Farmers accent! His words are written phonetically to help.
....

Narrator:
It is a well-known fact that many children would rather do anything than eat their vegetables. This makes it difficult to get children to be thankful for all the good things God provides and therefore this Harvest Festival play is all about the journey everyone goes through to realise the value of food. We do not have 18 years to do this - therefore we will be improvising with a Fairy God Farmer.

Mother:
Can you set the table for dinner, we are going to have a little celebration just the family, for harvest festival.

Florence:
What's Harvest Festival?

Mother:
Well where do you think all the food that we eat comes from every day.

Florence:
Morrisons?

Mother:
Well yes, in a way, but where do Morrisons get it from.

Florence:
Well, I don't know really.

Mother:
Well Florence, all the food is grown by farmers and Harvest Festival is when we give thanks to God for all the food he provides for us. It is at this time of year when the farmers gather in all the crops so that we have food to eat.

Florence:

So like fish fingers, beans and chips?

Mother:

No. I mean like potatoes, wheat, beans, peas and sprouts. Those kinds of things.

Florence:

But I don't like those things.
I like ice cream! – can we give thanks for ice cream?

Mother:

I suppose so now please set the table.

Narrator:

Like all good parents Mother does her best cooking for Florence for the Sunday lunch.
The celebration lunch is a roast – yum. Roast beef, Yorkshire pudding, roast potatoes,
roast parsnips, peas, sprouts and gravy.

Father:

Now Florence, eat up – it's all good for you.

Narrator:

Florence starts to eat the food she likes best.

Father:

Florence don't forget to eat your vegetables as well.

Florence:

But I hate sprouts – they are disgusting.

Mother:

They are not disgusting, they are lovely, healthy and good for you.

Father:

Florence, eat your sprouts now.

Florence:

Where is a Fairy God Mother when you need one?

Narrator:

As if by magic the Fairy God Farmer appeared

FGF

You called!

Florence:

Who are you?

FGF:

Oi'm the Fairy God Farmer – pleased to make your acquaintance.
OOOOOARRRRRRRRRR

Florence:

What happened to my Fairy God Mother?

FGF:

Meeting of the Fairy God Mothers Association. You got me and oi 'ave delegated authority to grant you 3 wishes.
OOOOOARRRRRRRRRR.

Florence:

Well I suppose you will have to do – can you make all the vegetables disappear so I never have to eat them again? Especially the sprouts?

FGF:

That oi can my dear but arrrrr you sure – life will be very bad.

Florence:

Definitely

FGF:

Allroight, your wish is granted.

Florence:

Wow that's amazing. Can you make chocolate take their place?

FGF:

Allroight, your second wish is granted. Don't forget to brush your teeth.

Narrator:

And with that the Fairy God Farmer disappeared.

Father:

Florence – eat your chocolates now! This is the last time I am going to ask you.

Florence:

Ok Dad. Look I'm eating them. Delicious. I actually love chocolates!

Mother:

Oh good girl Florence, you are such a good girl for finishing all your chocolates.

Narrator:

At first Florence thought she had been very clever however later, things were not turning out as she expected. Her favourite meal of fish fingers chips and beans was now fish fingers, chocolate and chocolate, vegetable soup was now chocolate soup, and bangers and mash was bangers and chocolate. Poor Florence. She felt sick most of the time and was putting on a lot of weight. Weeks turned into months, and months of very similar meals which were becoming less and less appealing.

Florence:

Why oh why did I make that stupid wish. I feel horrible. Maybe I could get the Fairy God Farmer back to get myself out of this mess.

Fairy God Farmer, Fairy God Farmer''

FGF:

Oi hope this is important, Oi was just in the middle o' sheering a sheep and was just at a tricky bit. The sheep will probably thank you though!

Florence:

Oh Fairy God Farmer, I have made silly wishes and I want things to go back to how they were. Can you help me – please??!

FGF:

Ahh well. Of course oi can moi dear. Don't forget you got one wish left – you've only had 2 wishes. You can wish things back to normal if you like but this is powerful magic and you need all the help you can get to put things back to normal. The more people who shout "The Fairy God Farmer is Cool" the better the magic will be.

Florence:

I am sure the congregation and the children will help me won't you?
After 3 we shout "The Fairy God Farmer is Cool"
1….2….,3…
{Congregation shouts the Fairy God Farmer is Cool}

Narrator: {in a superior tone of voice}

Ladies and gentlemen, now I hate to break it to you but there is no such thing as the Fairy God Farmer and there also NOT a pot of gold at the end of the rainbow. However, there is light at the end of this tunnel and the point is this:

Be grateful for what you have! THE END.

Harvest – Thank You Lord for the Corn

Resources:
Puppet theatre
1 male puppet
2 female puppets

Background:
A short play with a focus on giving thanks for the harvest. The song at the end is to the tune of "Sing Aloud" – have the choir support the children in this and you could even hand out song sheets to the congregation with the new words

....

Annie:
Well I've had a pretty good harvest this year - loads of tomatoes. The runner beans were good, and I'm getting plenty of apples off my tree now.

Bert:
Well I've grown potatoes this year and carrots. They've been great! But I did forget to pick my courgettes until after it had rained, and they ended up as the biggest marrows you've ever seen.

Annie:
I managed to pick loads of blackberries as well this year – they were really juicy. So, I've been pretty pleased with my efforts.

Bert:
I love strawberries. The local "Pick Your Own" now insist on weighing me before I go in and after I come out instead of weighing the punnet. The cheek of it!

Cathy:
Well everything I planted died. I went on holiday and asked my mother in law to water the plants. Apparently, the shopping was particularly good that week, so she didn't have time to fill a watering can. If there was a need for sun crisped tomatoes we would be fine! Months of care ruined in one week.

Annie:
Well you've got to be prepared to put the effort in…..

Cathy:
Like you and the blackberries you mean? Not exactly a lot of effort there on your part!

Annie:
I picked them, didn't I? I can't think of anyone else who made much of a contribution towards them.

Bert:

Really? We are in church you know. Can't you think of <u>anyone</u> else who may have helped with those blackberries? And your tomatoes, runner beans and apples too for that matter?

Annie:

Nope, all down to my own hard work.

Cathy:

You really can be pretty dense sometimes! We are in <u>church</u>. He is talking about <u>God</u>.

Annie:

Didn't see him taking on much of the back-breaking toil.

Bert:

But last week you were telling me that all the fruit this year was down to the prolonged cold snap and warmth and rain at the right time, and then the glorious sunny weather. Not exactly back-breaking toil on your part there.

Cathy:

Let's face it, you have had to do nothing towards the apples and blackberries – except go and pick what was provided and freely on offer.

Annie:

Well I did make them into a very nice apple and blackberry crumble…

Bert:

Luckily, I have written a song all about the things we grow and why sun crisped tomatoes are the exception to the rule that God provides everything we need….. Dah dah - dah dah.dah

Choir:♫

Thank you Lord, for the sun
We like food, everyone
Plants need rain to give grain
Melons grapes and carrots
Apples and bananas

Sing a harvest song, Sing a harvest song
Sing it out, sing it LOUD, Shout it from the tree tops

Thank you Lord for the corn
It will grow every morn
It gets threshed then gets ground
Ready for our breakfast
Crunchy nuts and cornflakes

Sing a harvest song, Sing a harvest song
Sing it out, sing it LOUD, Shout it from the tree tops

Thank you Lord for the wheat
And the fruit that we eat
Blackberries oh so sweet
Gathered from the hedgerows
Making every - thing. grow

Sing a harvest song, Sing a harvest song
Sing it out, sing it LOUD, Shout it from the tree tops

God gives food to us all
Listen hard, hear him call
Us to him, one and all
Thank him for the harvest
Thank him for the harvest

Sing a harvest song, Sing a harvest song
Sing it out, sing it LOUD, Shout it from the tree tops

Bert:
THE END.

Mothering Sunday – Supermum!!

Resources:

Puppet theatre
1 male puppet
2 female puppets

Background:

If a mother could be made by machine, what would be created. Nikki gets the opportunity to design herself a mother – with a little help from a couple of mad scientists. You will need a couple of props for this. An old computer keyboard and a box that can be opened from the front for the mummy to appear from.

....

Narrator:

Two scientists working in the lab try the ultimate challenge to make a mummy as the ultimate present for someone in need. They enlist the help of a young orphan girl.

Scientist 1:

So young lady, ready to start?

Nikki:

I can't wait, you can really make a mummy for me? So, what I say you will put into the machine and out she will come?

Scientist 2:

Well what will happen is that I will call out an attribute and you tell me (from what you know) the percentage it should be. I key it in and that's what you will get. The fabricator which makes your mummy will do the rest. {mad laugh}

Nikki:

That sounds easy enough. When do we start?

Scientist 2:

No time like the present. Let's start with an easy one – volume?

Nikki:

Well my friends say loud, really really loud like a sonic boom. Say 80%.

Scientist 2:

{tap tap tap} - done. What about patience?

Nikki:

Err not that high 10% say.

Scientist 2:
{tap tap tap} - done. What about irritability?

Nikki:
Medium especially when people forget things like PE kit or pick their nose and eat it or hang things up on the floordrobe. 50%.

Scientist 2:
{tap tap tap} - check. Anger?

Nikki:
Yes, sometimes in my experience say 20%.

Scientist:
and what about neuroses.

Nikki:
What are neuroses?

Scientist 1:
Well things that you worry about in respect of yourself, self-consciousness. Do I look fat in this dress? - that kind of thing.

Nikki:
Well that is _very_ high - happens all the time. 90%

Scientist 2:
So let's see what we have created so far.

Machine: {noises made}
Whizz, bang, bang whirr.

Monster: {appears out of upright box}
errrrrrrrrr,errrrrrrrrrrrr {mummy like puppet is deranged}

Scientist 1:
You idiots, you have not balanced it up or finished the attributes.
Quick get it back in! {puppets bundle the mummy back into the box}.

Narrator:
So Amy and the scientists continued through the night on the more positive attributes of a mummy like playing, caring, discipline, planning, mending, cooking, and kindness.

Scientist 2:

Do you know after all this work, we have forgotten something. Can anyone tell me what it is? It is probably the most important thing a mummy need to have - can someone in the congregation tell me what it is?

Congregation: {responds}

Love!

Scientist 2:

Yes that's right, love. I think love is the major one we still need to put in. 100% should be about right.

Scientist 1:

So let's see what we have created the second time - hopefully an improvement on the Mark 1.

Scientist 2:

{tap tap tap} - check.

Machine: {Noises are made}

Whizz, bang, bang whirr. *{a normal nice mummy appears out of the box}*

Nikki:

She's wonderful, thank you so much. It's the best Mothering Sunday present ever. THE END

Mothering Sunday – The Mothering Sunday Pirate!

Resources:
Puppet theatre
1 small parrot puppet
2 male puppets
2 female puppets

Background:
A mother always loves her son no matter what. And what's the matter with being a pirate – well having a parrot for one thing. The parrot is the comedy part in this play. The pirate is called Half Armed Pete so if you fold his left arm in two and put the parrot on the end of a metal puppet pole which is put through Pete's folded arm, the parrot can jump up and down on his shoulder. Make sure Pete is properly hammed up by someone who does a great pirate voice. When the parrot speaks, make sure it is parrot like. This one is a firm favourite with our church.

....

Narrator:
It was a dark and stormy night when Half-armed Pete, the local pirate, rolled back to his home turf with his faithful parrot by his side.

Half-Armed Pete:
Oo-ar! Scurvy knaves!

Percy Parrot:
Bandy-legged old coot!

Narrator:
Pete was happily rolling down the High Street, looking forward to seeing his dear ol' mum, when he saw a sign in a shop window.

{Shop assistant appears with 'Mothering Sunday' sign}

Percy Parrot:
Dragon ahoy!

Half-Armed Pete:
Mothering Sunday! Must do something about that; can't turn up empty handed to see me ol' mum after all these years at sea! *{To shop assistant}* Can I buy one o' yer cards – I'll gi' yer a gold coin stolen from a Spanish galleon?

Shop Assistant:
Ooh, I'd never know what the right change would be, and I could never accept stolen gold *{giggles}*.

Percy Parrot:

Give us a kiss?

Half-Armed Pete:

Right then, let's try the florist! Can I buy some o' yer flowers for me dear ol' mum, lovely Spanish gold here to pay for them?

Florist: {Posh Voice}

No stolen coins here please! Anyway, I'm just about to shut up and go home for the evening.

Percy Parrot:

Go and soak your dentures!

Narrator:

Half-armed Pete didn't know what to do. Every shop was either closing or didn't want his pirate gold. And after all those years away he really wanted to get something for his mum, who still loved him as much as she ever had, despite him being a terror of the seven seas.

Percy Parrot:

Percy needs a sick bag!

Half-Armed Pete:

Of course we could always have roast parrot instead of roast chicken for Sunday lunch?

Percy Parrot:

Who's a pretty boy then?

Half-Armed Pete:

That's better! Now, a gift for me dear ol' mum – those daffodils will do. Let's just swipe some of them and I can go around to see her.

Narrator:

But just as the deed had been done, a furious man emerged from his house, shaking his fist at Pete.

Man:

What are you doing with my prize daffodils?

Half-Armed Pete:

Sorry mate, sorry, but I didn't know what else to do. I've been away at sea and haven't seen my mum for years, and I can't go and see her on Mothering Sunday without taking her something. No one in town will sell me anything.

Percy Parrot:

Liar liar, pants on fire!

Half-Armed Pete:

Don't listen to him, I promise it's the truth! Look, here are some gold coins – will you take some for the daffodils?

Man:

That's alright, you take them – I'm sure your mum will appreciate them, and I'm happy to forgive you if they are for her. Don't worry about the money – I think you have enough to put up with that wretched parrot!

Half-Armed Pete:

Thank you matey.

Narrator:

So Half-armed Pete was able to take some flowers to his mum for Mothering Sunday. She was delighted with them, but it didn't stop her telling him what she thought of his life as a pirate. So, Pete gave away his Spanish gold to an animal sanctuary, on condition that they also took the parrot!
And they all lived happily ever after!

Mothering Sunday – Instructions for Mothers

Resources:
Puppet theatre
2 people puppets

Background:
Imagine a Mother came with an instruction manual (don't we all wish that!). From a child's perspective this would be invaluable and that is what this play is all about. We hope it brings a smile to your face. The song at the end is to the tune of "Sing Aloud".

....

Narrator:
Wouldn't it be good if Mothers came with a handbook so that life would run just a little bit smoother. We thought so too, so we have written a play about how the Mother works; some of the common mistakes that can be made and how to avoid them. Enjoy.

Puppet 1:
This guide if followed closely will provide for many years of happy Mothers.

Puppet 2:
Let's take a typical day. When a Mother says "time to get up", what she really means is if I can't have the extra half an hour in bed, then no one else is going to. The condition is called "Shared Insomnia" but is not contagious. The condition is severely aggravated, if the mother is greeted with persistent and fake snoring.

Puppet 1:
A particularly sensitive time of the morning is at breakfast. At this time of day (and despite what you were taught the previous day by your mother), honesty is not the best policy! At breakfast time you are allowed to be extremely generous with compliments. You can complement hair, skillfully applied make up, moderate temperament and fashion sense. The mother should not be asked about weight, colour coordination or Polyfilla.

Puppet 2:
A kiss for your mother should always be applied prior to departure and before the front door opens. This indicates that the mother is much loved and provides happy fuel for the mother for the day. The alternative is for the Mother to apply the kiss to the child outside of the house and comments like "Muuuumm - don't" and "Gerrof" are merely providing ammunition for the Mother for the end of the day. This should be avoided because a Mother has an extremely long memory and does not forget rather like the elephant.

Puppet 1:

Upon returning to the house, it is a good idea to ensure that you do not leave a trail of destruction behind you. Casually discarded bags, crockery and shoes in the hall or kitchen cause the mother to get into a mode called "The Warpath". The Warpath is largely acknowledged to be like a cloud that may take many hours to disperse.

Puppet 2:

At this point it is relevant to mention the Brownie Point system. Points are mentally added or taken away from the child based on performance. The higher the number of points on the Brownie scale, the happier the mother is. Brownie points are best attained towards the end of the day as tiredness sets in for the mother. In this way, Brownie points earned in the evening are worth more than those in the afternoon which are in turn worth more than those in the morning.

Narrator:

Actions which earn Brownie points:

Puppet 1:

Making the mother a hot or cold drink upon return to the house.

Puppet 2:

Asking how the Mother's day has been.

Puppet 1:

Getting the Mothers slippers for her.

Puppet 2:

Asking if there is there is anything you can do for her.

Narrator:

Actions which lose Brownie points:

Puppet 1:

Forced - but amusing bodily noises.

Puppet 2:

Walking through the house - after walking through a field of cows.

Puppet 1:

Leaving unwanted sandwiches under the bed for 3 months - to see if they can grow fur

Puppet 2:

Putting your ironing away on the floor.

Puppet 1:

During the evening, it is customary to eat dinner. Mothers come in a range of cooking abilities from Michelin starred to Primordial Soup Preparation - from which life emerges. In the event, the Mother comes from the school of Primordial Soup preparation, it is inadvisable to do anything with it except try to swallow it and then try to smile - as opposed to re - presenting it on the table cloth.
Feeding it to the dog should also be avoided as vet's bills are expensive these days.

Puppet 2:

However, there is one day in the year that we just say thank you to our Mothers because they deserve it and they are great. In line with this tradition we conclude with our Mothering Sunday song. Maestro, if you please.

♫

In the morn, we arise
mum is there, no surprise
working hard in our lives
feeding us our breakfast
makes us sure and steadfast
She is always there,
Always there to care,
We give thanks, to the Lord, for her loving kindness.

At the end of the day
Shapes our lives, every way
What we do, what we say
Where she constantly strives
Happiness in our lives,
She is always there,
Always there to care,
We give thanks, to the Lord, for her loving kindness.

Narrator:

So, to all our Mothers wherever they are, Happy Mothering Sunday.
THE END

Pentecost – The Holy Spirit Quiz

Resources:
Puppet theatre
1 Puppet

Background:
Ever wondered what your Priest thinks about Pentecost. Now is the chance for you to find out and spring this one on him/her. It is better if it is spontaneous because then it becomes very interactive as opposed to being your Priest giving considered answers. Have someone in the audience prepared to shout "Fail and we eat it for you!" Have someone ready to put a seat right in front of the congregation for the priest to sit on.

....

Annie:
Hello everyone, and welcome to the Holy Spirit Quiz!

Congregation {Cheers}

Annie:
So, this is the show that chooses someone from the audience to answer questions about the Holy Spirit. And today --PAUSE --- [Name of Priest...................] this is your lucky day! Come on up - don't be shy; I don't bite - unless provoked!

{a member of the congregation place a seat facing the congregation}

Here is the hot seat!
Do you have insulation? (no?).
Well never mind -- asbestos trousers are so hard to find these days.

Now the rules are these:
1. one sentence answers only, and
2. you cannot answer with Yes or No.

Clear?

Congregation - these are all genuine questions asked by members of your Sunday School. [Name of Priest.....................] - answer them all correctly and you win this lovely bar of chocolate.

Member of congregation: {shouts}
Fail and we eat it for you!

Annie:
So, [Name of Priest], are you ready?

{Priest responds}

Annie:

So [Name of Priest], why does the Holy Spirit come to us?

{Priest responds}

Annie:

Great answer, onto the next question.

Question 2:Where is the Holy Spirit today?

{Priest responds}

Annie:

You are on form today [Name of Priest], onto the next question.

Question 3:What does the Holy Spirit do for me?

{Priest responds}

Annie:

Seriously. 3 out of 3. We thought we would be breaking open the chocolate by now. Next question - are you ready?

Question 4:
Is the Holy Spirit part of God?

{Priest responds}

Annie:

I can see us losing our chocolate soon! Please don't deprive the lovely children (smile and stare for 4 seconds)

Question 5:
How long will the Holy Spirit stay for?

{Priest responds}

Annie:

Well let's just check the final score if we can!

Congregation Member

[Name of Priest] scored full marks!

Congregation

Yeah!!! (Applause)

Annie:

Well done [Name of Priest] on winning this delicious bar of chocolate. And we'll see you all next time on The Holy Spirit Quiz - when it may be <u>your turn</u> in the hot seat!
THE END.

Pentecost – Pentecost Live

Resources:

Puppet theatre
6 people puppets, 1 animal puppet (donkey), all but one person with small cardboard flames pinned onto their heads

Background:

What if a reporter started to try to interview people who had the Holy Spirit suddenly come upon them. Confusion – you bet!

....

Interviewer:

Hello, I am speaking to you live from Jerusalem, where the strangest events have been unfolding. People are walking around saying the strangest things, with large flames coming out of the top of their heads! I am going to try and speak to one or two of them, and see if I can get any sense out of them! Excuse me madam, would you talk to me?

Puppet 1:

Bonjour! Comment ca-va?

Interviewer:

Not very helpful! Sir, maybe I could ask you?

Puppet 2:

Hola! Com es das?

Interviewer:

What? – never mind!

Donkey:

Eeyore!

Interviewer:

Will somebody get this donkey out of the way? He really isn't helping!

Donkey:

Well thank you very much lady, I thought everyone knew I was the brains around here! Huh!

Puppet 3:

Guten Tag! Wie gehts'?

Interviewer:
This is now doing my head in? Why can't I understand what is going on? Madam, can you…

Puppet 4:
Ciao! Come siete?

Interviewer:
Aaargh! Sir, can you explain to me what is going on?

Puppet 5:
Yes, I certainly can! You see we were all together, when the Holy Spirit came upon us!

Others:
Oui/ Si/ Ja/ Si/ Eeyore {at the end}

Interviewer:
How so?

Puppet 5:
Well it came down on us as tongues of fire.

Others:
Oui/ Si/ Ja/ Si/ Eeyore *{at the end}*

Puppet 5:
When the Spirit came down we suddenly found that we had the power to speak other languages we had never known before. It was an amazing feeling.

Others:
Oui/ Si/ Ja/ Si/ Eeyore *{at the end}*

Interviewer:
So what is going to happen now?

Puppet 5:
We are going to use this great gift God has given us and go out to tell the good news about Jesus to other countries.

Interviewer:
So there we have it folks, good news coming somewhere near you, and in your own language too. So goodbye for now.

Others:
Au revoir/ Adios/ Auf wiedersehn/ Ciao/ Goodbye/ Eeyore! THE END.

The Prodigal Daughter

Resources:

Puppet theatre
3 female puppets, 2 male puppets

Background:

This is a modern day rewriting of the prodigal son. It makes it more relevant in today's world and something that the children can relate to. The narrator can speak from a microphone away from the theatre.

....

Narrator:

We start our story on Christmas Day morning and brother and sister Bill and Becky are just opening presents. Bill is 16 and Becky is 14 years old. Needless to say, teenage strops are now an everyday occurrence.

Mum:

Now Becky and Bill I am just going to make your father some coffee then we'll sit down to open all our presents.

Bill:

I'll do that for you Mum after all it is Christmas Day and you are doing all the dinner.

Becky:

I don't know what all the fuss is about, it's just another day like every other day.

Dad:

Well no it is isn't, it's the day we celebrate when Jesus was born and important for lots of reasons.

Bill:

Yes and we get lots of presents so let me go and sort out the coffee while you sort out the presents into piles.

Becky:

Well I only asked for money so I'm not going to get much in the way of presents anyway.

Dad:

But that's what you asked for so that you could get lots of nice things in the sales.

Narrator:
So Mum sorted out the presents into piles. There was a giant pile for Bill, a medium size pile for Mum, a tiny pile for Dad (as usual – probably handkerchiefs anyway) a pile of cards for Becky.

Becky:
See, see. All of you have got lots of presents and I haven't got anything except a pile of cards. It's not fair – how come Bill has all that lot and I have nothing.

Dad:
Why don't you open your cards and then you will see what everyone has bought you.

Narrator:
15 minutes later all the presents have been opened.

Bill:
I can't believe I got all these things; iPod, new mobile phone and best of all a tablet. This is the best Christmas ever….

Dad:
Handkerchiefs and pants – fantastic!

Mum:
Thanks for the spa day darling.

Becky:
I have got £300 – I have plans for this!!

Dad:
At least we'll get some peace and quiet now.

Narrator:
So Becky laid out plans for a fashion consultancy. After Christmas, she cleared her bank account went shopping in the sales and bought everything she needed for her new venture. This largely consisted of:

3 pairs of platform shoes (pink)
2 pairs of corduroy flares (orange)
1 tank top (purple)
3 wing collar shirts (white)
And a flamboyant scarlet hat

Becky:
Right, now all I need are some customers.

Dad:

I think you may be making something of a large assumption here Becky.

Becky:

What's that then Dad.

Dad:

That people will want to take your advice on fashion.

Becky:

Of course they will – that is really rude Dad!

Dad:

Just trying to help and by the way – how much did you spend on that lot?

Becky:

Err, I have got about £2.50 left.

Dad:

Out of what?

Becky:

Everything I had.

Dad:

What – you're joking! You have put all your money from Christmas into this business?

Becky:

Yes – and it's going to be fantastic.

Mum:

So how many customers have you got.

Becky:

Well I'm just starting so at the moment, only one.

Mum:

Oh that's excellent darling and who is that?

Becky:

My best friend Sarah – she's coming around for some advice tomorrow.

Narrator:

The next day Sarah comes around for her fashion consultation.

Sarah:

I'm not wearing that – I'll look like a clown. I suppose you haven't got a big red nose to go with the big floppy shoes, have you?

Becky:

I'm a consultant you know – anyway my fee for my advice will be £30 please.

Sarah:

You want me to pay you £30 to look like the biggest fashion disaster since Elton John. I'm off – goodbye!

Mum:

So how did it go darling?

Becky:

Oh mum, I think I've made a terrible mistake. Sarah thought my advice was stupid and didn't pay for it. Worse, she thought I had Elton John's fashion sense. I've spent everything – everything from all my Christmas's and Birthdays. All those gifts have been wasted.

Mum:

Oh – I see. Well I'm sure your Dad will be able to give you a good lecture on this but why don't we do this. Why don't you take all those lovely clothes down to the Fancy Dress shop in town and see if you can get them to buy them from you. At least you can see if you can get some of your money back that way and then we'll come back and have your favorite dinner to cheer you up.

Becky:

You're not angry?

Mum:

Well, we all do silly things occasionally – the main thing is that we learn from our mistakes and know what's important and what isn't. So, we just have your Dad to convince of that now.

Narrator:

So Becky learnt that nothing is as important as forgiving. THE END.

The Trinity

Resources:
Puppet theatre
3 people puppets
1 T Shirt

Background:
God knows what's happening – quite literally. When a person is ready to make the admittance to Holy Communion or Confirmation – God knows why. He lets us know by the actions of the person and what the person says. This play reflects an imagined narrative by the Trinity. In our play, we got an old adults T Shirt, and cut 3 holes for the heads of three puppets to go through – you'll see why!! This play will need to be adapted according the event and the names of the people going through the sacrament.

....

Father:
Well – here we all are. Where is he/ she *or* are they? {looks around then looks pointedly at the person being confirmed}. Hello [Names] {pause}. You look nice! {pause}. Are you nervous? {pause} You should be! Right off we go. Ladies and gents, you may not know this but [Names} have been studying hard so that he/she/they can take [sacrament]. Anyway, today we have a puppet play which I know you will all love. Be warned – audience participation required.

Holy Spirit:
So who is on the list today. Anyone special?

Son:
Ohhh yes. [Names]. {flicking through paper} No, no that's my list of the criminally insane, a reminder to pick up my shroud from the launderette. Are here we are. Yes - stars for the day and the main event.
Excepting me of course!

Father:
I sense some confusion in the congregation. For the sake everyone present, we need to explain who we are. You there! – Vicar! – have a guess! {after the guess either say "that's right" or "nope" – then say "that one is Holy Spirit {takes a bow}, that one is my son {takes a bow}, and I am the Father {takes a bow}. {Says slowly} And why are we all in one of the Churchwardens old T Shirts Vicar? {after the guess either say "that's right" or "nope" – then say "because we are one body -yeeeessss.

Holy Spirit:
Technically - being the holy spirit, I don't need a body but I do get around a bit.....

Son:
{interrupts} but seriously, how do we know if he/she/they, is/are ready? It's a big step.

Holy Spirit:

As I was about to say. I get around a bit and I was sitting in on one of [Names] confirmation/ First Communion lessons. He's/she's/they're very good you know!

[PUT YOUR OWN ANECDOTES IN HERE INSTEAD]:
Example: Fiona was talking about badges and that everyone gets a badge when they first join the church. She asked Emily if she knew what badge she has and do you know what Emily said? She said without any prompting that she got a badge when she was baptized and was signed with the cross on her forehead with oil.

Is he/she ready? {laughs} – are you ready for him/her/them more like!! VICAR?

Father:

Every week, he/she/they have been completing their preparation work you know. He/she/they now knows why we are important and everything. Of course, Son here gets the biggest airplay but we are all involved.

Son:

Yes, bread and wine are central to Holy Communion. The bread being my body and the wine being my blood because no one goes to my Father except through me. But all three of us are important in Holy Communion. I am the body of the Christ, the Holy Spirit is like the soul and my Father is like the mind which understands everything regardless. Like all fathers, he is difficult to understand which is why he gave you his Son – {says very slowly} to translate for you.

Father:

They understand all that at their age!

Spirit:

Mostly yes - but they don't need to. After all, not everyone understands things in the same way. As long as they are spiritually ready then that is the most important thing. And of course, they aren't on this journey alone. They have their families to help them. They have [names of ministers]. Are you still with us VICAR? –. In fact, they have everyone in this church to help them on their journey – and that started when they were baptised.

[For use in First Communion
Son:
And after this, their next major milestone on their journey will be Holy Confirmation.]

Father:

And all along their journey, he/she/they will now recognize the face of God in the people around him/her/them who look out for him/her/them, care for him/her/them, support him/her/them and help him/her/them grow in faith.

Son:

So congregation - will you help him/her/them?

Congregation:

{a few will answer yes}

Son:

So reserved – are they English?

Father {booms}:

Louder - He said, will you help him/her/them on their journey?

Congregation:

YES

Son:

So – we better get on with it.

Over to you Vicar. Are you still with us - VICAR? Are yes - up you come. Well done every one, well done. Carry on.

29830748R00061

Printed in Poland
by Amazon Fulfillment
Poland Sp. z o.o., Wrocław